THE DECADENT
BESTIARY

THE
DECADENT
BESTIARY

❧

Fin-de-siècle
Animal Poems & Prose

Selected and Translated by
SAM KUNKEL & **JESSICA GOSSLING**

To Ziggy, Georges, Kafka, and Nefertiti

THE DECADENT BESTIARY

SELECTED AND TRANSLATED BY
Sam Kunkel & Jessica Gossling.

FIRST PUBLISHED BY
Strange Attractor Press in 2025,
in an unlimited paperback and
a limited hardback edition of 300 copies.

LAYOUT & COVER DESIGN BY
Tihana Šare and Baphorock.

Ouroboros linocut by Baphorock.

TYPESET IN
Delvard Serif & Bestiary.

ISBN: 9781917674041

A CIP CATALOGUE RECORD for this book
is available from the British Library.

DISTRIBUTED BY The MIT Press, Cambridge,
Massachusetts. And London, England.

PRINTED AND BOUND IN Estonia by
Tallinna Raamatutrükikoda.

STRANGE ATTRACTOR PRESS
BM SAP, London, WC1N 3XX UK,
www.strangeattractor.co.uk

Acknowledgements

We would like to extend our thanks to the academics, creatives, and decadents who inspired us at various stages of this project: Nicole G. Albert, Alice Condé, Michael P. Daley, Jane Desmarais, Guy Ducrey, Karl Hatton, Tim Jarvis, James Machin, Clémence Pilleur, and Évanghélia Stead.

Contents

BIRDS

FISH & HERPTILES

INSECTS & ARACHNIDS

EPILOGUE: HUMANS

I never reared a young Wombat
    To glad me with his pin-hole eye,
But when he most was sweet & fat
And tail-less, he was sure to die!

Beasts of Beauty and Burden

SAM KUNKEL & JESSICA GOSSLING

In a letter to his mother, Charles Baudelaire, the godfather of decadence, complained that it was impossible to live with his mistress Jeanne Duval because she had 'turned out the cat, my only pleasure in the house, and [...] brings in dogs *because* the sight of them makes me ill'.[1] Baudelaire's love for cats permeates his poetry, in which felines are often described as sensual and mystical, but also as symbols of rebellion and non-conformity. Baudelaire's cats are both profane and sacred — a contradiction that runs through his poetry, as well as the later blossoming of the decadent literary tradition at the fin de siècle. Indeed, as the reader shall soon see, the decadent animal is bicephalic, incarnating multiple — often contradictory — traits beneath the transformative gaze of the writer.

'Decadence', with its etymological connections to the Latin word *decidere* [a falling away] — from *de-* 'off, away' and *cadere* 'to fall' — refers to a state of decline or deterioration, often associated with a perceived moral, cultural, or societal decay. In different contexts, decadence can manifest as an excessive indulgence in luxury, pleasure, or self-gratification, leading to a weakening or breakdown of social and moral norms. *Decidere* also has a cyclical connotation, as it is at the root of 'deciduous' — what we call trees whose leaves fall each autumn — and 'decadent' is similarly used to describe a period of history marked by a decline or a fall in moral standards. As a critical concept, decadence is characterized by excess, artificiality, and a departure from traditional values. It can be observed in various aspects of human life, including literature, art, philosophy, and social behaviour, reflecting a departure from established norms or ideals, and is not delineated by time, place, or culture.

Decadence is, in many ways, a literature of distance. Although they take different forms and have different sources, the stories and poems that make up the canon of decadent literature depict an essential rupture between the author and the world surrounding them. Unable to relate to a society populated by individuals who are unwilling or unable to share the same point of view, the decadent writer turns their back on the world around them and embraces personal experiences that hold an entirely private meaning. While for some decadent protagonists this means a total rejection of the common experience of the material world and a retreat into a realm of artifice, others, as this collection illustrates, choose to maintain a relationship with the real in the form of a connection with an entirely different realm: the animal kingdom.

The irony of a collection of decadent animal stories and poems is that animals, and nature more generally, cannot be decadent. Decadence is a human concept tied to excess and moral decay, often involving conscious moral agency, and predominantly associated with human artifice — dandyism, consumerism, and a life lived *à rebours*. It is thus culturally subjective, rooted in the mores and values of a given society, and encompasses uniquely human complexities, rendering it unsuitable for describing the behaviours of non-human species. Animals lack this moral reasoning and act primarily on instinct. Their behaviours, though perhaps more extravagant than our own in appearance, serve natural intuitions rather than societal or moral considerations. However, it is precisely the animal's inability to engage critically or rationally that often makes it an object of fascination for the decadent writer, who sees in it something that is completely outside of oneself, untamable and beyond logical classification. The reaction provoked by this essential unknowability varies drastically from writer to writer, ranging from awe to abjection. The decadent attitude doesn't simply negate nature, but beckons it into a complex dance. It interrogates the very essence of what is considered natural in a landscape dominated by human intervention, and this introspective juxtaposition challenges conventional perceptions, forcing a re-evaluation of the boundaries between the natural and the artificial, the wild and the tame, the animal and the human.

Des Esseintes' Tortoise: A Martyr for Decadence

Sparked in the 1880s as a reaction to the realism of the Naturalist movement, which was perceived as depicting only the superficiality of modern life, the decadents of the 'yellow 90s' used their works to glorify everything that was left behind: the monstrous, the beautiful, the excessive, and the rare. It is interesting, then, to consider the relationship between the decadent author and the animal, which, as the reader will see, is far from uniform. The distance that is essential to their writing is consistent, but it manifests itself in different ways. For some, the animal is a reminder of their inescapable mortality and their place in the natural order; for others, the animal becomes an object of yearning and aspirational beauty, a reminder that there are spheres of grace and loveliness beyond the tedium of the common world. However, this epiphany is often accompanied by the sentiment that that beauty and grace is no longer meant for them — and perhaps never was.

Decadence and animals exist in a multifaceted and often enigmatic relationship that reflects the interplay between human civilization and the natural world. Domesticated creatures, such as Baudelaire's cat, are a perfect example of this liminality due to their intermediary status between untouched nature and human-controlled environments.

However, other, arguably stranger, examples can be found as well. In Chapter Four of the breviary of decadence, Joris-Karl Huysmans' novel À rebours [*Against Nature*] (1884), des Esseintes' only pet, a tortoise, makes a brief appearance:

> This tortoise was a fancy which had come to des Esseintes some time before his flight from Paris. One day, as he examined an Oriental rug, in reflected light, and followed the silver gleams which ran the length of its wool, plum violet and Aladdin yellow, he remarked to himself how good it would be to place some object upon it whose deep colour might heighten the vivaciousness of its tints.[2]

The tortoise is a perfect example of des Esseintes' excessive and luxurious taste, which seeks to improve on nature to the point of destruction. Following his purchase of the tortoise, des Esseintes quickly decides to turn it into an art

object itself by gilding its shell and encrusting it with rare gemstones. Initially selected so as to heighten the visual impact of an oriental rug, the pet tortoise lives for only an afternoon before being crushed to death by the weight of its gilded and bejewelled shell:

> He touched it; it was dead. Most likely accustomed to a sedentary existence, to a humble life spent beneath a modest shell, it had been unable to bear the dazzling luxury imposed upon it, the rutilant cape in which it had been clad, the gemstones with which its back had been paved, like a ciborium.[3]

Ultimately, the curatorial impulses of Huysmans' protagonist kill the animal. In order to elevate the tortoise to the level of an art object within the larger artistic context of an immaculately-curated collector's house, des Esseintes subjects the animal to a series of costly and unnatural metamorphoses in the name of beauty. The tortoise becomes a conscripted victim, unwillingly sacrificed upon the altar of aesthetics. However, his elevation of a common animal to the status of a luxury object also enables us to draw an interesting distinction between the decadent treatment of animals and that of their Naturalist contemporaries — namely those depicted by Émile Zola.

Known for his gritty and aggressively realistic depictions of life, Zola shocked readers with his 1887 novel *La Terre* [*The Earth*], which included long passages not only detailing the work of livestock on a farm, but also lengthy and graphic descriptions of their copulation. Upon publication, the novel sparked a firestorm of controversy, with severe repercussions in both France and England. In France, five young novelists, who had once prided themselves on being disciples of Zola, penned a scathing manifesto which they published in *Le Figaro*, breaking away from him and suggesting that he seek treatment in an asylum for his 'morbid obsessions'. It was the publication of this essay, known as 'Le Manifest des cinq', that in many ways sounded the death knell of the French naturalist school. Similarly, when the first English translation appeared in 1888, the publisher, Henry Vizetelly, was sued for obscenity.

Des Esseintes' tortoise is, essentially, a decadent Shield of Achilles — just as the shield is a symbol for the art of war, so the tortoise's shell illustrates the importance of beauty and collection in the life of the decadent artist and how nature can serve as a conduit for decadent taste. However, the martyred tortoise is a decadent animal not just because of its synthetic and curated beauty, but for its relationship to des Esseintes. Like Baudelaire's cat, which is an extension of the liminal position of the poet, des Esseintes sees in his tortoise a double of himself. His treatment of it is a complete rejection of conventional ways of being and a dedication to a life lived as art even to the point of death — ultimately both des Esseintes and the tortoise are suffocated by a life of luxury and excess.

Curating a pet to match one's carpet may seem like nothing more than an odd, nineteenth-century fantasy, but in Huysmans's writing, we can see a playful development of a long-standing fashion common among the European bourgeoisie and royalty for keeping pedigree and exotic animals as curated companions. Members of the nobility had certainly enjoyed keeping pets in various capacities for some time, but with the nineteenth century came a growing infatuation for it among ordinary citizens, marking a departure from the traditional role of domestic animals as purely functional or utilitarian beings towards the contemporary desire for pets as fashion accessories and expressions of personal taste.

As trade routes became more developed, international transport easier, and private individuals able to amass great amounts of wealth for the first time, they were also able to acquire animals foreign to Europe. Writers such as Dante Gabriel Rossetti, for example, were drawn to these more unusual animals and had unfettered access to them thanks to Charles Jamrach, who ran an exotic pet shop on the Ratcliffe Highway, East London, and supplied Londoners with rare birds and mammals — including a tiger that once escaped and an elephant that Rossetti almost bought, declining only because the price was too high. Rossetti was famous for keeping a small menagerie in his garden, which included a wombat named Top, whose untimely demise he immortalized in an illustrated poem, depicted at the beginning of this introduction.

At the end of the nineteenth century, animals also began to play a surprising role in contemporary fashion. A feature in an 1898 issue of the French revue, *L'Illustration*, the images from which are reproduced on pages 18 and 19 of this book, advertised the sale of live baby turtles with a gold ornament attached to their shells, to be worn as pendants on special occasions. Indeed, the article, which includes an interview with the retailer responsible for selling them, describes how they are especially popular with women who belong to the fashionable and artistic *demi-monde*. Although it is debatable whether such a thing is a mere coincidence, the article describes the fashion as a uniquely French creation and 'a sign of our decadence'—all but confirming that the trend finds its origin in the unfortunate tortoise who came to meet his end at the house at Fontenay-aux-Roses.

A Bestiary of Decadence or a Decadent Bestiary?

Throughout history, changes in our understanding and perception of animals have been driven by cultural and intellectual trends as well as advances in scientific knowledge and fluctuations in religious or philosophical beliefs. The bestiary, or 'book of beasts', is a compendium of animals that reflects these developments. Popular in northern Europe throughout the Middle Ages and derived from early Christian morality tales and classical reflections on the natural world, the first bestiaries contained anywhere from a few dozen to a hundred descriptions of animals, each accompanied by a representative image. These real and imaginary creatures were imbued with symbolic connotations by their authors, and their descriptions illustrated virtues, vices, or moral lessons.

The thirteenth-century *Ashmole Bestiary*, which contains one hundred and thirty miniature drawings in its one hundred and five pages, and the luxurious *Aberdeen Bestiary* (1582), with its expertly-painted illustrations and lavish use of gold leaf, are two prominent examples of the medieval obsession with nature and the cultural fascination with the mysterious and the divine. During the Renaissance, a renewed interest in classical literature sparked a revival in bestiary creation. This period also saw a shift from purely symbolic interpretations to a greater emphasis on scientific inquiry, resulting in more accurate depictions of the natural world that reflected the developing field of zoology and empirical observation.

This shift continued to grow and swell throughout the eighteenth and nineteenth centuries, where it was bolstered by a resurgence of interest in natural history and the classification of species, driven in part by the development of evolutionary theory. While there is no distinct genre of Victorian bestiary comparable to those of earlier eras, there were certainly works produced during the nineteenth century that incorporated elements reminiscent of bestiaries in their exploration of the natural world — albeit with a more scientific approach. In France, for example, Louis Buffon's eighteenth-century text, *Histoire naturelle, générale et particulière*, admirably attempted to compress the flora and fauna of the natural world into a comprehensive, knowable format, which spanned no fewer than thirty-six volumes. However, though such texts were certainly extensive in their breadth, they lack allegorical or moralising elements, focusing rather on empirical, positive categories, and thus mark a significant departure from the true bestiaries that preceded them.

While the number and type of animals represented in a given bestiary could vary greatly — some even featured rocks — and the contents could be configured in many different ways, a bestiary is undeniably a decadent artefact. This position derives first and foremost from the extravagance of the bestiary's physical form: replete with ornate illustrations, thick, expensive paper and luxurious bindings, a bestiary is an object that only a select group of individuals could afford, and, because its contents are a synthesis of a wide range of literary, artistic, and philosophical elements, it is also a book intended to be read and understood by a limited number of people. Bestiaries are a testament to the opulence and sophistication of the cultures that produced them, reflecting a desire to explore and interpret the natural world through a lens of beauty, symbolism, and moral significance. As bestiaries have been produced consistently over multiple centuries, there is no set format for what they should contain. Rather, they reflect the choices of their authors, who are, of course, products of their own age and culture. In this collection we have brought together forty-two animal stories and poems by *fin-de-siècle* decadents and symbolists writing in both French and English — the largest number ever assembled — alongside artwork from natural history textbooks and private collections. In the spirit of the traditional bestiary, we have focused on collecting complete stories and poems where animals are the central concern and have excluded brief mentions of creatures when they appear momentarily in a longer narrative, however iconic.

Decadent writing is grounded in reality, but often presents a distorted or heightened version of it, where the boundaries between the tangible and the fantastic are blurred, and this is true of the animals in this collection. Mystical and mythical creatures rarely feature in decadent writing, largely due to its focus on enhanced, real-world experiences. Instead, real creatures are shown as occupying a space between the real and imaginary, as in Saki's 'Sredni Vashtar' (1912), or are drawn into dream-like worlds, such as in Eric Stenbock's 'The Egg of the Albatross' (1894). At the centre of this imaginative oscillation is the human animal, depicted as navigating a maze of desires and contradictions in which the non-human animal serves as a symbol of the absurdity of existence and the individual's struggle for meaning and connection in a seemingly indifferent universe. While stories such as Rachilde's 'The Frog Killer' (1900) depict the barbaric aspects of man, in the epilogue to our collection, 'A Friend to the Animals' (1897), this existentialism is expressed in moral terms by Léon Bloy, who posits that a return to a morally sound existence will coincide with a realignment with animals and that it is our duty to act as their stewards. This story reflects a shift in consciousness that emerged following Charles Darwin's challenge, in *The Descent of Man* (1871), to the notion of a divide between humans and animals and the superiority of humans over 'lesser' creatures. Decadent writers of the fin de siècle grapple with this increasingly urgent conceptualisation of humanity as no longer very different from the animal.

Ultimately, our aim in *The Decadent Bestiary* is to show how the decadent writer does not renounce nature but celebrates it in all its forms — as beautiful and familiar, perverse and strange — and to illustrate the types of animal-human relationships that we find in *fin-de-siècle* decadent writing. In this way, it serves as a kind of guide to animals as they may be encountered in other works of decadent fiction. For medieval readers, the bestiary helped to reinforce the notion that the natural world was created by God to instruct mankind, and we hope that our decadent readers will read this collection as an homage to and parody of the bestiary as a didactic tool. In a traditional medieval bestiary, the lion, known as the 'king of the beasts', is placed first, and the ant, the smallest and most commonplace animal is placed last. We have followed this convention by beginning this collection with Victor Hugo's spectacular poem 'To Androcles' Lion' (1859), which revisits and inverts the feline figure first featured in Aesop's fable wherein a lion with a thorn stuck in his paw is helped by a human, and ending with Lafcadio Hearn's 'The Dream of Akinosuké' (1904), in which ants are depicted as part of a complex and tragic dynasty rather than as servile and prosaic workers coming together for the common good. From the lion through to the ant, decadent writers present beasts of beauty and burden, an imaginative sympathy and a kinship as instinctive as it is inevitable.

ENDNOTES

1   Charles Baudelaire to his mother, 27 March 1852, *The Letters of Charles Baudelaire to his Mother, 1833–1866*, trans. by Arthur Symons (J. Rodker, 1929), p. 45. Original italics.
2   Joris-Karl Huysmans, *À rebours* (A. Ferroud. – F. Ferroud, 1920), p. 43. Translated by Sam Kunkel.
3   Huysmans, p. 53.

BEASTS

To Androcles' Lion

VICTOR HUGO

The city was the image of the heavens.
That hour when all souls fall silent, reverent,
When the world changes, and the stars expire.
Rome had stretched its purple out over the mire.
Where the eagle had flown, now buzzards did glide,
Trimalchio trod the bones where Scipio died,
Rome drank, gay, drunken and its face stained red;
While from the orgy rose the scent of the dead.
Love and happiness, all was pretext for dread,
Lesbia sat smiling, her hair perfect on her head,
As at her feet, Catullus watched with an amorous stare,

If the Persian slave with her fine braids took care,
Or pricked her pale breast with his needle of gold,
Evil in the soul of man had taken hold;
Pleasures grew lewd for they were now unrestricted.
Swift deaths by sons unto fathers were inflicted.
Rhetoricians denounced tyrants before the dumb.
It was the age of gold and mud. In dungeons dim, glum,
Executioners violated saints with hate.
Horrible Rome sang its song. As, before its gates,
Crassus, the conqueror of slaves and kings, did ride
That great road lined with enemies each crucified,
And, when Catullus, the lover who now hears this song,
Walked that road with Delia, far from Rome's great throng,
Six thousand human trees bled upon their love,
Rome, first showered with glory sent from above,
Now saw itself beset by great shame and scorn,
Messalina laughed as she laid bare her pale form,
And stretched out, lying down upon the bed of the whore.
Epaphroditus, who took men as toys when bored,
Broke the limbs of Epictetus while thrashing, wild.
A large woman, an old man, a breastfeeding child,
Captives, gladiators, Christians, all were cast,
Into the pits with the beasts, trembling, scared, aghast,
And there, quivering, for the spectator's delight,
They howled and screamed, writhing in a circus of fright.
And as echoing growls sounded from beasts and bears,
And elephants trampled children caught unaware,
The vestal did dream upon her white marble throne,
And death, like fruit on the branch of a tree fresh grown,
Fell from the pensive brow of that pale beauty;
The same flash of dark sin and savage duty,
Leapt from the eye of the tiger to the pale maiden.
The world was the wood, the empire the haven.
Dark passers-by found their way to the throne,
Took their seat, and gnawed mankind down to the bone,

Then they left. Nero came after Tiberius.
Cesar trod o'er the Huns, the Goths, the Iberians;
And the emperor, like flowers that bloom for a brief time,
Withered like a corpse for he was not divine.
The vile Vitellius rolled down the Gemonian stairs,
Where the low and high alike dare not to err,
Pillory of the void, jail of souls uncompliant,
Bleeding, rotting, putrid, that carnal house of giants,
Seemed to cause the skeleton of the earth to decay,
Men groaned on that hill 'neath the heat of the day,
Tongueless Jews, eyeless bandits, handless thieves;
Just as in that circus there raged ceaselessly
An agony, crying out with every single step.
The great black gulf opened its archway in the depths,
And Rome sank in; and, there within that great sewer,
When just Heaven smote with lightning the wrongdoers,
Sometimes two emperors, part of that sad, final few,
Would meet, still alive, and there, cast in drab hues,
In places where dogs come to strip bones of their flesh,
Today's Cesar put his predecessor to death.
Grim crime had become the lover of vice most dark,
In place of that race wherein God had lain his spark,
In place of Adam and Eve, so pure and so fair,
A coiled hydra held the universe ensnared;
Man, woman, a bicephalic beast with one blood.
Rome was the mother sow wallowing in the mud.
The human creature cast a pallor in the sky,
Pulling a dark shadow over God's great eye;
It no longer resembled its initial form;
It rumbled and sparked like black clouds in a storm,
And we saw, on the eve of Atilla's advance,
All that had been held as holy fall to mischance,
On one side the virtues writhing beneath his claw,
On the other the glories dangling from his jaw.
Struggling to speak, Man's cheeks grew red.

Humanity's soul yearned to flee, stricken with dread;
But, before leaving this sad world full of fault,
She hesitated and trembled, beneath that starry vault,
And sought out a great beast, wherein she might hide,
Man could hear the tomb, as it called and cried.
Beneath, pale Death laughed, his eyes cruel and alert.
And so it was but you, born in the distant desert,
Where one finds not but the sun, God, and star-filled nights,
Who came from that lair filled with the sun's slanting light,
To this place, a crowded, heaving den of thieves,
Shivering, filled all with dread and uncertainty;
Your eye swept over this castigated city,
Showering it thereof with love and pity,
And pensive, upon great Rome did you shake your mane,
And, o Lion, with you being the man, 'twas Man the beast in pain.

The Lady with the Wolf

RENÉE VIVIEN

Told by M. Pierre Lenoir, 69, rue des Dames, Paris.

I do not know why I endeavoured to court that lady. She was neither beautiful, nor pretty, nor even pleasant. While as for myself (I will remind my female readers that I say this with no self-satisfaction), my looks have been remarked upon, from time to time. It is not that I was extraordinarily blessed by Nature in the realms of physical or moral attributes: but, well — dare I say it? — such as I am, I have been extremely spoiled by sex. Oh! Rest assured: I am not going to subject you to some vain tale of my conquests. I am a man of modesty. Furthermore, this is not about me, in fact. It is about that woman, or rather about that young lady, it is about that English girl whose curious face pleased me for an hour or so.

She was a strange being. When I drew near to her for the first time, a great beast was sleeping in the dragging folds of her skirt. I had, upon my lips, those pleasantly banal words that facilitate relations between strangers. The words themselves are nothing in such an instance — their power resides in the manner of their oration...

But, raising its muzzle, that great beast growled in a sinister way, just as I approached that seductive stranger.

I took a step back, despite myself.

"That's quite a mean dog you have, mademoiselle,"

I observed.

"She's a wolf," she responded, dryly. "And, because sometimes her aversions are as violent as they are inexplicable, I think you would do well to keep your distance."

"Helga!" she called sternly, and her wolf fell silent.

I stepped back in retreat, somewhat humiliated. You have to admit: it was a silly story. I do not know fear, but I hate ridicule. The incident bothered me all the more because I thought that I had detected a gleam of sympathy in the young woman's eyes. I certainly pleased her to some extent. She must have been as disappointed as I over that regrettable incident. What a pity! The conversation had started so well!...

I don't know what prompted that horrible animal to cease its hostile manifestations. I was later able to approach its owner without fear. Never before had I seen such a strange thing. Beneath her heavy hair, which was a blonde like red ashes, both ardent and sallow, was the paleness of her complexion. Her emaciated body had the fine, frail, delicateness of a beautiful skeleton. (All of us Parisian men are a bit artistic, you see.) That woman's demeanour suggested a harsh and solitary pride, of flight and furious withdrawal. Her yellow eyes resembled those of her wolf.

They had the same gaze of dark hostility. Her steps were so silent that it was a cause for concern. No one had ever walked with so little sound. She was dressed in a thick fabric that resembled fur. She was neither beautiful, nor pretty, nor charming. But, that said, she was the only woman on board.

And so, I courted her. I observed the most solidly-established rules pertaining to time-honoured tradition. She had the cleverness to keep the deep pleasure that my advances caused her hidden from me. She even managed to maintain that same defiant expression present in her yellow eyes. An admirable example of feminine ruse! The sole result of that manoeuvre was to make me feel an even more violent attraction towards her. Lengthy resistances can sometimes be the cause of pleasant surprises, and make victory even more dazzling... Gentlemen, surely you are in agreement with me on this? We all have more or less the same feelings. Between us there is a spiritual fraternity so complete that it makes conversation nearly impossible. That is why I often flee the monotone company of men, for they are too similar to myself.

Decidedly, the Lady with the Wolf attracted me. And, need I confess it? The confined chastity of those floating jails exasperated my tumultuous senses. She was a woman... And my courtship, which had been respectful up to that point, became more urgent with each passing day. I accumulated enflamed metaphors. I also elegantly cultivated periods of eloquence.

You can see how far the treachery of that woman went! She assumed, as she listened to me, a near lunar aloofness. One would have said that she was interested solely in the froth of the ship's wake, which was like smoking snow. (Women are highly sensitive to poetic comparisons.) But myself, who am a long-time student of the psychology perceptible on the face of a woman, I understood that her lowered eyelids concealed flickering glimmers of love.

One day, moved by audacity, as I sought to unite flattering gestures with delicate words, she turned to me, leaping like a wolf.

"Get out of here," she ordered with an almost savage resolve. Her teeth, like those of a wild animal, shone strangely beneath her curled lips.

I smiled unconcernedly. You have to have a lot of patience when it comes to women, don't you agree? And you must never believe a single word of what they say. When they tell you to leave, you have to stay. In truth, gentlemen, I am slightly embarrassed to be saying such banal things to you.

She considered me with her large, yellow eyes.

"You have not understood me. You have only hurled yourself against my unflinching disdain. I am incapable of both love and hate. I have never met a human being worthy of my hate. Hate, which is more patient and tenacious than love, demands a worthy adversary."

She stroked the heavy head of Helga, who contemplated her with her deep, feminine eyes.

"As for love, I am entirely unaware of what it is just as you are unaware of what it means to hide the complacency inherent to men — which is elementary to us other Anglo-Saxons. If I were a man, I would have perhaps loved a woman. For women possess the qualities that I admire: loyalty in passion and loss of self in tenderness. They are simple and sincere, for the most part. They give of themselves without restrictions and without calculations. Their patience is unflagging, as is their goodness. They know how to forgive. They know how to wait. They possess that superior chasteness which we call: constancy."

I possess finesse in excess, and know how to read in-between the lines. I smiled purposely at that explosion of enthusiasm. With a distracted glance, she saw right through me.

"Oh, you are strangely mistaken! I have seen women who were very generous of spirit and heart. But I never let myself become attached to them. Their very softness kept them from me. My soul was not yet high enough to not become impatient before their excessive candour and devotion."

She was starting to bother me with her pretentious speeches. She was as prude and bookish as she was shrill!... But she was the only woman on board... And furthermore, she only adopted those superior airs so as to render her future capitulation all the more precious.

"I have affection only for Helga. And Helga knows it. As for you, you are no doubt a fine young man, but you cannot imagine the degree to which I despise you."

She sought, in irritating my pride, to exacerbate my desire. She was succeeding, as well, that little minx! I was red with rage and lust.

"Men who crowd around women, regardless of who the women are, are like dogs sniffing after potential mates."

She cast one of her long, yellow, stares in my direction.

"For so long, I breathed the air of the forests, air that vibrates, alive with the snow, I so often melded myself with the vast, deserted Whiteness, that my soul is a bit like the soul of bounding wolves."

After all of this, the woman frightened me. She noticed it and changed her tone.

"I love cleanness and freshness," she continued with a light laugh. "However, the vulgarity of men repels me like the stench of garlic, and their uncleanliness pushes me away like a gust of fetid air rising from a sewer grate. A man," she insisted, "is only himself when he is in a brothel. He loves only courtesans. For in them, he finds his own rapaciousness, his own sentimental unintelligence, his own stupid cruelty. He lives only for self-interest or debauchery. Morally, he sickens me; physically, he repulses me... I have seen men kiss women on the mouth while groping them obscenely. Even a gorilla would act in a less repellent manner."

She stopped for a moment.

"It is only by a miracle that the most austere legislator manages to escape from the maddening consequences of the carnal promiscuities which occurred during his youth. I do not understand how the most delicate of women manage to withstand your kisses without retching. In truth, my virgin scorn is matched only by the nausea of the courtesan in disgust."

Decidedly, I thought, she is exaggerating her role, which she clearly understands quite well. She exaggerates.

(If we were among only men, Gentlemen, I would tell you that I did not always despise public houses and that I had even, upon numerous occasions, scooped up pitiful birds from the sidewalk. That does not stop the women of Paris from being more accommodating than this holier-than-thou woman. I am not trying to be pretentious, but one must have a realistic understanding of one's worth, when all is said and done.)

And, having decided that the conversation had gone on for long enough, I left the Lady with the Wolf in the most dignified of manners. Helga, glowering, followed me with her long, yellow, stare.

...Clouds heavy like towers appeared on the horizon. Above them, a bit of dark green sky writhed like a serpent. I had the impression of being crushed beneath a heavy wall of stones...

And the wind rose...

Seasickness gripped me... I would ask that my female readers forgive this inelegant detail... I was horribly indisposed... I finally fell asleep around midnight, more lamentable than I could ever say.

Towards two in the morning, I was awakened by a sinister shock, followed by a grinding which was even more sinister still... Shadows stole all about in an indescribable horror. I understood, finally, that the ship had run aground upon a reef.

For the first time of my life, I neglected my appearance. I emerged upon the deck in an outfit which was altogether forgettable.

A crowd of men, half-nude, was already there, shoving one another... They were lowering the lifeboats as quickly as they were able.

Seeing those arms and those hairy legs and those woolly chests, a smile came across my face, and I couldn't help but think of something the Lady with the Wolf had said: *"Even a gorilla would act in a less repellent manner."*

I do not know why, in this midst of this great peril, that silly memory came to mock me.

The waves resembled monstrous volcanoes enveloped in white smoke. Or rather, no, they did not resemble anything. They were themselves, magnificent, terrible, mortal... The wind blew upon that boundless rage and exacerbated it further. The salt bit at my eyelids. I shivered beneath the spray, as if beneath a fog. And the great din of the sea smothered any thought that may have developed within me.

The Lady with the Wolf was calmer than ever. And I was weak with fear. I saw Death rise before me. I almost touched him. With a dazed hand, I patted my forehead where I felt the bones of my skull protrude horribly. My own skeleton horrified me. Stupidly, I began to cry...

I was to become a mass of black and blue flesh, more swollen than a wineskin. Sharks would encircle me from all about, snapping at my disjointed members. And when I descended to the depths, crabs would scuttle obliquely across my rotting body and feast gluttonously upon it...

The wind blew upon the sea...

I saw the past once more. I repented for my imbecilic life, for my wasted life, for my spoiled life. I wanted to recall a blessing accorded to me by distraction or happenstance. Had I ever been useful to someone, good for something? And my dark conscience cried out within me, horrible like a mute woman who has suddenly recovered the gift of sound:

"No!"

The wind blew upon the sea...

Vaguely I recalled the holy words that beckoned to repentance and promised, at the very hour of agony, the salvation of the penitent sinner. I tried to recall, from the depths of my memory, emptier than a drained glass, a few words of prayer... And libidinous thoughts came to torment me, like red demons. I saw anew the sullied beds of my disparate partners. I heard anew their stupidly obscene cries. I conjured anew the loveless embraces. The horror of Pleasure gripped me.

Before my fright at that Mysterious Vastness, the only thing that survived within me was the instinct of breeding, which is as powerful for some of us as that of self-preservation. It was Life, the ugliness and boorishness of Life, that bellowed within me in a ferocious protest against Annihilation...

The wind blew upon the sea...

One thinks strange thoughts in moments such as those... Myself, an honest man, to be sure, well-esteemed by all, save for by several jealous individuals, loved even by some, blaming myself with such bitterness for an existence which was neither better nor worse than that of everyone else!... I must have had a passing spell of madness. We were all a bit mad, then...

The Lady with the Wolf, quite calm, was watching the white waves... Oh! Whiter than the snow at dusk! And, seated upon her flanks, Helga was howling like a dog. She howled a lamentation, like a dog at the moon... She *understood*...

I do not know why these howls did more to freeze me than the noise of the wind and the waves... She howled unto death, that wild devil-wolf! I wanted to hit her so she would stop, and I was looking for a plank, a spar, an iron rod, anything really to put her down right there on the deck... I found nothing...

The lifeboat was finally ready to leave. Men bounded furiously towards their salvation. Alone, the Lady with the Wolf stood immobile.

"Well, climb aboard already," I cried out to her as I took my seat.

Unrushed, she moved nearer, followed by Helga.

"Mademoiselle," interrupted the lieutenant who was doling out orders, "we cannot take that animal with us. We only have space for humans."

"Then I will stay," she said, coldly...

Panicked people pressed forward, shouting incoherently. We were forced to let her drift away.

As for me, I found myself incapable of summoning any embarrassment for a harlot such as her. And especially one who had been so insolent to me! You can understand that, can't you, gentlemen? You would not have acted differently than I did.

Finally, I was saved, or something close to it. The dawn rose, and what a dawn, my God! It was a shivering, penetrating light, a grey stupor, a growling of beings and of larvae-like things in a twilight of limbs...

And we saw the distant land grow blue...

Oh! The joy and the comfort that came from the sight of the sound, welcoming, land!... Since that horrible experience, I have taken only one single journey at sea, to return here. And I shall never take another!

I must be a bit selfish here, Ladies. In the midst of the unspeakable uncertainty in which I was debating, and despite having narrowly escaped Destruction, I still had the courage to wonder about the fate of my companions of misfortune. The second lifeboat had been submerged by the frenetic assault of an exceedingly large number of panicked people. With horror, I saw it sink... The Lady with the Wolf had taken refuge upon a broken mast, a floating wreck, along with her submissive beast... I was certain that, if the strength of that woman's endurance held, she could be saved. I wished for it with all my heart... But the cold, the slowness, and the fragility of that improvised embarkation, with no sails and no rudder, the fatigue, the feminine feebleness!

...They were but a short distance from the land, when the Lady, exhausted, turned to Helga, as if to say, "I'm at my end..."

And then a painful and solemn thing happened. The wolf, *who had understood*, cast out to the nearby, unreachable, shore its howl of despair... Then, rising, she placed her two front paws upon the shoulders of her mistress, who took her in her arms... Both then sank beneath the waves...

Pierrot

GUY DE MAUPASSANT

To Henry Roujon

Mrs Lefèvre was a woman of the country, a widow, one of those half-country women dressed in ribbons and sun hats, one of those people who add unnecessary syllables to their words, adopt grandiose airs in public, and harbour the soul of a pretentious beast beneath their comic and decorated exteriors, just as they hide their large, red hands within gloves of raw silk.

Her servant was a simple, hearty countrywoman named Rose.

The two women lived in a little house with green shutters, along a road, in Normandy, in the middle of the Caux countryside.

Because in front of the domicile, they had a narrow garden, they grew vegetables.

But, one night, someone stole a dozen onions from them.

As soon as Rose noticed the theft, she ran to alert Mrs Lefèvre, who came down in a wool skirt. Both were stricken with desolation and terror. They stole, they stole, Mrs Lefèvre! There were thieves in the area, and they could come back.

And the two frightened women contemplated the footprints, chatting, imagining things: "Look, they must have gone through there. They put their feet on the wall: they jumped in the flower bed."

And they feared for the future. How ever could they sleep soundly now?

News of the theft spread. The neighbours came, took note, and discussed among themselves — and the two women explained, to each new person who came, their observations and their ideas.

A farmer from nearby offered a piece of advice: "You should get a dog."

That much was true: they should get a dog, if only to wake them up with its barking. Not a big dog, heavens! What would they do with a big dog? The cost of food alone would ruin them. But a little dog (in Normandy they pronounce it *deg*), a little, yappy furball of a *deg*.

Once everyone had left, Mrs Lefèvre discussed the idea of a dog for a long time. After consideration, she made a thousand objections, terrified by the image of a dish full of wet food: for she was one of those parsimonious sorts of countrywomen who always carry coins in their pockets so that they can clearly and ostentatiously offer one to any beggar they might encounter along the road, and add one to the collection plate on Sunday.

Rose, who liked animals, presented her arguments and defended the idea cleverly. And so it was decided that they would get a dog, a very small dog.

They began to look for one, but only found big ones, great soup-gulpers who would make a person shudder. The shopkeeper in Rolleville had one, however — a small one; but he asked that they buy him for two francs, to pay back the money he had already spent on raising it. Mrs Lefèvre declared that she would feed a *deg*, but she would not buy one.

But, the baker, who knew what had taken place, brought, one morning, in his car, a strange little yellow animal, nearly pawless, with a body like a crocodile, a head like a fox, and a tail curly like a trumpet, like an ostrich feather, and just as long as the rest of his body. A client was looking to get rid of him for free. Mrs Lefèvre found the filthy runt quite handsome. Rose kissed him, then asked what his name was. The baker answered, "Pierrot."

They made him a bed in an old soapbox and gave him first some water to drink. He drank. Then they gave him a piece of bread. He ate. Mrs Lefèvre, worried, had an idea: "When he is used to the house, we'll let him roam free. He'll find food foraging out in the countryside."

Indeed, they let him roam free, which did not stop him from being famished. And he only yapped when he wanted scraps; but when that happened, he yapped with vigour.

Anyone could go into the garden. Pierrot went to nuzzle each newcomer, and remained absolutely silent.

Mrs Lefèvre, however, had grown accustomed to the animal. She even came to love him, and, from time to time, to let him eat mouthfuls of bread soaked in the grease of her fry-up from her hand.

But she had never considered the taxes she was to incur, and when they asked her to pay eight francs — eight francs, Madame! — for that runt of a *deg* who had never barked once, she nearly fainted in shock.

It was immediately decided that they had to get rid of Pierrot. No one wanted him. All of the houses, for ten leagues in each direction, turned him down. So, they decided, for lack of a better solution, to have him "move out to the hut."

"Moving out to the hut" means "eating chalk." People have their dogs "move out to the hut" when they want to get rid of them.

In the middle of a vast field, there is a strange sort of hut, or rather, a tiny little thatched roof, placed on the ground. It's the entrance to the pit of a chalk quarry. A large well that goes straight down twenty meters beneath the ground, before branching off into a long series of mining galleries.

People go down into that quarry once a year, at the same time as people marl the fields. The rest of the time, it acts as a cemetery for condemned dogs; and often, when people pass near the orifice, plaintive howls, desperate or furious barks, lamentable cries, rise up from the earth.

The dogs of the hunters and the shepherds flee in terror when they come too close to that gaping hole; and, when you bend over it, the awful stench of rotten things comes out.

Horrible things play out in its shadows.

When an animal lies in agony for ten or twelve days in that cavern, surviving upon the disgusting remains of its predecessors, a new, bigger, and certainly more vigorous, animal is suddenly thrown in. And there they stay, alone, famished, their eyes gleaming. They eye one another, following one another, hesitating, anxious. But hunger weighs upon them; they attack, wrestling at length, feral; the strongest eats the weakest, devouring him alive.

When it was decided that they would have Pierrot "move out to the hut," they looked into finding an executioner. The roadman who was hoeing the road said that he would do it for ten sous. That seemed unreasonably steep to Mrs Lefèvre. The neighbour's boorish husband said that he would be happy to do it for only five sous, but this was still too much; and, with Rose having made the observation that it would be better that they carry him themselves, because that way he wouldn't be beaten along the way and alerted to what awaited him, it was decided that the two of them would go, once it was dark.

That evening, they gave him a nice soup with a healthy dose of butter. He drank it down to the last drop; and, because he was wagging his tale in contentment, Rose took him in her apron.

They walked quickly across the plain, like two marauders. Soon the thatched roof appeared in their sight, and they came to it; Mrs Lefèvre bent down to make sure that she didn't hear the sound of a whimpering animal. No — there wasn't one: Pierrot would be alone. And so, Rose began to cry, kissed him, and then threw him into the hole; and then both bent over, listening attentively.

First they heard a muted sound; then the sharp, piercing, whimpering of a wounded animal, then a succession of painful little cries, then the desperate calls and begging yaps of a beseeching dog, whose head was raised towards the opening.

He yapped, oh! how he yapped!

They were stricken with horrible regret, with a wild, inexplicable, fear; and they fled running. And, because Rose was faster, Mrs Lefèvre called out: "Wait for me, Rose, wait for me!"

Their night was haunted by horrible nightmares.

Mrs Lefèvre dreamt that she was sitting at a table to eat soup, but when she found the soup pot, Pierrot was inside. He sprang out and bit her on the nose.

She awoke and thought that she heard more yapping. She listened; she had been mistaken.

She fell asleep again and found herself upon a great road, an endless road, that she walked. Suddenly, in the middle of the path, she noticed a basket, the big basket of a farmer, abandoned; and this basket scared her.

Nevertheless she managed to open it eventually, and Pierrot, curled inside, grabbed hold of her hand, and did not let go; and she fled blindly, carrying on the end of her arm the suspended dog, his jaw clamped tight.

At daybreak, she woke, near mad, and ran to the chalk quarry.

He was yapping; he was still yapping, he had yapped all night long. She began to sob and called to him with a thousand sweet nicknames. He responded with all of the tender inflections of his canine voice.

And so she wanted to see him again, swearing to herself that she would make him happy for the rest of his days.

She ran to the home of the well worker who was responsible for extracting the chalk, and she explained the situation to him. The man listened without saying a word. When she had finished, he said, "Yeh want yer deg? It'll cost yeh four francs."

She jumped, startled: all of her pain suddenly left her body.

"Four francs! You can go die! Four francs!"

He responded: "Yeh think I'm g'nna bring my ropes, my cranks, set all that up, and g'down there with my boy and get bit again by yer rotten little deg, just for the fun o' givin' him back to yeh? Shouldn't a thrown him in."

And she left, indignant.

Once she was back, she called Rose and told her of the well worker's pretentiousness. Rose, still resigned, repeated: "Four francs! That's a tidy bit of money, madame."

Then, she added: "What if we threw some food to that poor deg, so that he doesn't die of hunger?"

Mrs Lefèvre approved, joyfully; and they set off again, with a large piece of buttered bread.

They cut it into bite-sized pieces that they threw one after another, calling to Pierrot each time they did so. And just as soon as the dog had finished one piece, he began yapping to demand another.

They returned that evening, then the next day, every day. But they only made one trip each day.

🐾 🐾

But one morning, when they dropped the first piece, they suddenly heard a formidable bark from within the well. There were two of them! Someone had thrown in another dog — a big one!

Rose cried out: "Pierrot!" And Pierrot yapped, yapped. And so they began to throw food: but, each time they did, they heard the clear sound of a horrible scuffle, and then the plaintive cries of Pierrot who had been bitten by his companion, who was eating everything, being the stronger.

They had made sure to specify: "This one's for you, Pierrot!" But Pierrot, apparently, received nothing.

The two women, puzzled, looked at one another; and Mrs Lefèvre, with a sour tone, said "I can't be expected to feed every single dog that gets thrown in there. We'll have to give up."

And, overwhelmed by the thought of all the dogs she would have to keep alive, she left, munching upon what was left of the bread as she walked.

Rose followed her, dabbing at the corners of her eyes with her blue apron.

With Dog and Dame: An October Idyll

A L E I S T E R   C R O W L E Y

The ways are golden with the leaves
That Autumn blows about the air,
The trees sing anthems of despair,
And my fair mistress binds the sheaves
Of yellow hair more loose, and weaves
More subtly bars of song, that bear
Bright children of love debonair,
And laughter lightly comes, and reaves
The garland from our sorrow's brow,
Life rises up, is girt with song,
Joy fills the cup, that flashes clear.
The year may fade in whispers now,
Shadow and silence now may throng
The seasons — we are happy here.

Autumn is on us as we lie
In creamy clouds of latticed light
That hint at darkness, but descry
A rosy flicker through the night,
My mistress, my great Dane, and I.

We linger in the dusk — her head
Lolls on the pillow, and my eyes
Catch rapture, as upon the bed
He licks her lazy lips, and tries
To tempt her tongue. My fires are fed.

Her heavy dropping breasts entice
My teeth to jewel them with blood,
Her hand prepares the sacrifice
She would desire of me, the flood
That wells from shrines of Paradise.

Her other hand is mischievous
To bid the monster Dane grow mad,
His red-haw gaze grows mutinous,
Her eyes have lost the calm they had,
My body grows all amorous.

My tongue within her mouth excites
Her dirtiest lust, her vilest dream;
His greedy mouth her bosom bites;
He cannot hold, his eyeballs gleam;
He burns to consummate the rites.

I yield him place: his ravening teeth
Cling hard to her — he buries him
Insane and furious in the sheath
She opens for him — wide and dim
My mouth is amorous beneath.

Her lips devour me, and I rave
With pleasure to discern the love
They twain exert, my lips who lave
With doubled dew distilled above;
To dog and woman I'm a slave,

Nor move, though now essays the Dane
To cool his weapon in my mouth;
Her lust bestrides me, and is fain
To quench in his sweet sweat her drouth
Her finger probes my bowel again.

All three enjoy once more, and I
Am ready ever to renew
These bestial orgie-nights, whereby
Loose woman's love is spiced, as dew
On tender spray of spring doth lie.

Like the cold moon to earth and sun
My mistress lingers in eclipse,
We wake her passion, either one
Licking each pouting pair of lips
Till new sweet streams of nectar run.

'Tis Autumn, and the dying breeze
Murmurs "embrace"; the moon replies
"Embrace"; the soughing of the trees
Calls us to linger loverwise,
And drain our passion to the lees.

'Tis Autumn. The belated dove
Calls through the beeches, that bestir
Themselves to kiss the skies above,
As I will kiss with him and her.
Leave us, sweet Autumn, to our love.

The Greyhound

IWAN GILKIN

For Georges Picard

The Scottish greyhound whose wild fur hangs in waves,
Accompanies in the morning garden his mistress,
Shuddering beneath the soft breath of her kisses,
As dreams of her light touch fill his pale gaze.

On the rug of her room at the close of each day,
His lithe figure stretched in arrogant excess,
Beneath his queen's feet he swoons with sweetness,
And licks her heels, savouring pleasure depraved.

And, his eyes populated with captive thoughts,
In the horror of silence, invisible and fraught,
He dies slowly, ruined by secret evil.

And so too do poets, with strange loves in their heads,
Overcome by an impossible, sublime ideal,
Expire, their hearts filled with words ever unsaid.

The Hound

H. P. LOVECRAFT

In my tortured ears there sounds unceasingly a nightmare whirring and flapping, and a faint, distant baying as of some gigantic hound. It is not dream — it is not, I fear, even madness — for too much has already happened to give me these merciful doubts.

St John is a mangled corpse; I alone know why, and such is my knowledge that I am about to blow out my brains for fear I shall be mangled in the same way. Down unlit and illimitable corridors of eldritch phantasy sweeps the black, shapeless Nemesis that drives me to self-annihilation.

May heaven forgive the folly and morbidity which led us both to so monstrous a fate! Wearied with the commonplaces of a prosaic world, where even the joys of romance and adventure soon grow stale, St John and I had followed enthusiastically every aesthetic and intellectual movement which promised respite from our devastating ennui. The enigmas of the Symbolists and the ecstasies of the pre-Raphaelites all were ours in their time, but each new mood was drained too soon of its diverting novelty and appeal.

Only the sombre philosophy of the Decadents could hold us, and this we found potent only by increasing gradually the depth and diabolism of our penetrations. Baudelaire and Huysmans were soon exhausted of thrills, till finally there remained for us only the more direct stimuli of unnatural personal experiences and adventures. It was this frightful emotional need which led us eventually to that detestable course which even in my present fear I mention with shame and timidity — that hideous extremity of human outrage, the abhorred practice of grave-robbing.

I cannot reveal the details of our shocking expeditions, or catalogue even partly the worst of the trophies adorning the nameless museum we prepared in the great stone house where we jointly dwelt, alone and servantless. Our museum was a blasphemous, unthinkable place, where with the satanic taste of neurotic virtuosi we had assembled a universe of terror and decay to excite our jaded sensibilities. It was a secret room, far, far underground; where huge winged daemons carven of basalt and onyx vomited from wide grinning mouths weird green and orange light, and hidden pneumatic pipes ruffled into kaleidoscopic dances of death the lines of red charnel things hand in hand woven in voluminous black hangings. Through these pipes came at will the odours our moods most craved; sometimes the scent of pale funeral lilies, sometimes the narcotic incense of imagined Eastern shrines of the kingly dead, and sometimes — how I shudder to recall it! — the frightful, soul-upheaving stenches of the uncovered grave.

Around the walls of this repellent chamber were cases of antique mummies alternating with comely, life-like bodies perfectly stuffed and cured by the taxidermist's art, and with headstones snatched from the oldest churchyards of the world. Niches here and there contained skulls of all shapes, and heads preserved in various stages of dissolution. There one might find the rotting, bald pates of famous noblemen, and the fresh and radiantly golden heads of new-buried children.

Statues and paintings there were, all of fiendish subjects and some executed by St John and myself. A locked portfolio, bound in tanned human skin, held certain unknown and unnamable drawings which it was rumoured Goya had perpetrated but dared not acknowledge. There were nauseous musical instruments, stringed, brass, and wood-wind, on which St John and I sometimes produced dissonances of exquisite morbidity and cacodaemoniacal ghastliness; whilst in a multitude of inlaid ebony cabinets reposed the most incredible and unimaginable variety of tomb-loot ever assembled by human madness and perversity. It is of this loot in particular that I must not speak — thank God I had the courage to destroy it long before I thought of destroying myself.

The predatory excursions on which we collected our unmentionable treasures were always artistically memorable events. We were no vulgar ghouls, but worked only under certain conditions of mood, landscape, environment, weather, season, and moonlight. These pastimes were to us the most exquisite form of aesthetic expression, and we gave their details a fastidious technical care. An inappropriate hour, a jarring lighting effect, or a clumsy manipulation of the damp sod, would almost totally destroy for us that ecstatic titilation which followed the exhumation of some ominous, grinning secret of the earth. Our quest for novel scenes and piquant conditions was feverish and insatiate — St John was always the leader, and he it was who led the way at last to that mocking, that accursed spot which brought us our hideous and inevitable doom.

By what malign fatality were we lured to that terrible Holland churchyard? I think it was the dark rumour and legendry, the tales of one buried for five centuries, who had himself been a ghoul in his time and had stolen a potent thing from a mighty sepulchre. I can recall the scene in these final moments — the pale autumnal moon over the graves, casting long horrible shadows; the grotesque trees, drooping sullenly to meet the neglected grass and the crumbling slabs; the vast legions of strangely colossal bats that flew against the moon; the antique ivied church pointing a huge spectral finger at the livid sky; the phosphorescent insects that danced like death-fires under the yews in a distant corner; the odours of mould, vegetation, and less explicable things that mingled feebly with the night-wind from over far swamps and seas; and worst of all, the faint deep-toned baying of some gigantic hound which we could neither see nor definitely place. As we heard this suggestion of baying we shuddered, remembering the tales of the peasantry; for he whom we sought had centuries before been found in this self-same spot, torn and mangled by the claws and teeth of some unspeakable beast.

I remember how we delved in this ghoul's grave with our spades, and how we thrilled at the picture of ourselves, the grave, the pale watching moon, the horrible shadows, the grotesque trees, the titanic bats, the antique church, the dancing death-fires, the sickening odours, the gently moaning night-wind, and the strange, half-heard, directionless baying, of whose objective existence we could scarcely be sure.

Then we struck a substance harder than the damp mould, and beheld a rotting oblong box crusted with mineral deposits from the long undisturbed ground. It was incredibly tough and thick, but so old that we finally pried it open and feasted our eyes on what it held.

Much — amazingly much — was left of the object despite the lapse of five hundred years. The skeleton, though crushed in places by the jaws of the thing that had killed it, held together with surprising firmness, and we gloated over the clean white skull and its long, firm teeth and its eyeless sockets that once had glowed with a charnel fever like our own. In the coffin lay an amulet of curious and exotic design, which had apparently been worn around the sleeper's neck. It was the oddly conventionalised figure of a crouching winged hound, or sphinx with a semi-canine face, and was exquisitely carved in antique Oriental fashion from a small piece of green jade. The expression on its features was repellent in the extreme, savouring at once of death, bestiality, and malevolence. Around the base was an inscription in characters which neither St John nor I could identify; and on the bottom, like a maker's seal, was graven a grotesque and formidable skull.

Immediately upon beholding this amulet we knew that we must possess it; that this treasure alone was our logical pelf from the centuried grave. Even had its outlines been unfamiliar we would have desired it, but as we looked more closely we saw that it was not wholly unfamiliar. Alien it indeed was to all art and literature which sane and balanced readers know, but we recognised it as the thing hinted of in the forbidden *Necronomicon* of the mad Arab Abdul Alhazred; the ghastly soul-symbol of the corpse-eating cult of inaccessible Leng, in Central Asia. All too well did we trace the sinister lineaments described by the old Arab daemonologist; lineaments, he wrote, drawn from some obscure supernatural manifestation of the souls of those who vexed and gnawed at the dead.

Seizing the green jade object, we gave a last glance at the bleached and cavern-eyed face of its owner and closed up the grave as we found it. As we hastened from that abhorrent spot, the stolen amulet in St John's pocket, we thought we saw the bats descend in a body to the earth we had so lately rifled, as if seeking for some cursed and unholy nourishment. But the autumn moon shone weak and pale, and we could not be sure. So, too, as we sailed the next day away from Holland to our home, we thought we heard the faint distant baying of some gigantic hound in the background. But the autumn wind moaned sad and wan, and we could not be sure.

II.

Less than a week after our return to England, strange things began to happen. We lived as recluses; devoid of friends, alone, and without servants in a few rooms of an ancient manorhouse on a bleak and unfrequented moor; so that our doors were seldom disturbed by the knock of the visitor.

Now, however, we were troubled by what seemed to be frequent tumblings in the night, not only around the doors but around the windows also, upper as well as lower. Once we fancied that a large, opaque body darkened the library window when the moon was shining against it, and another time we thought we heard a whirring or flapping sound not far off. On each occasion investigation revealed nothing, and we began to ascribe the occurrences to imagination alone — that same curiously disturbed imagination which still prolonged in our ears the faint far baying we thought we had heard in the Holland churchyard. The jade amulet now reposed in a niche in our museum, and sometimes we burned strangely scented candles before it. We read much in Alhazred's *Necronomicon* about its properties, and about the relation of ghouls' souls to the objects it symbolised; and were disturbed by what we read.

Then terror came.

On the night of September 24, 19 —, I heard a knock at my chamber door. Fancying it St John's, I bade the knocker enter, but was answered only by a shrill laugh. There was no one in the corridor. When I aroused St John from his sleep, he professed entire ignorance of the event, and became as worried as I. It was that night that the faint, distant baying over the moor became to us a certain and dreaded reality.

Four days later, whilst we were both in the hidden museum, there came a low, cautious scratching at the single door which led to the secret library staircase. Our alarm was now divided, for besides our fear of the unknown, we had always entertained a dread that our grisly collection might be discovered. Extinguishing all lights, we proceeded to the door and threw it suddenly open; whereupon we felt an unaccountable rush of air, and heard as if receding far away a queer combination of rustling, tittering, and articulate chatter. Whether we were mad, dreaming, or in our senses, we did not try to determine. We only realised, with the blackest of apprehensions, that the apparently disembodied chatter was beyond a doubt *in the Dutch language*.

After that we lived in growing horror and fascination. Mostly we held to the theory that we were jointly going mad from our life of unnatural excitements, but sometimes it pleased us more to dramatise ourselves as the victims of some creeping and appalling doom. Bizarre manifestations were now too frequent to count. Our lonely house was seemingly alive with the presence of some malign being whose nature we could not guess, and every night that daemoniac baying rolled over the windswept moor, always louder and louder. On October 29 we found in the soft earth underneath the library window a series of footprints utterly impossible to describe. They were as baffling as the hordes of great bats which haunted the old manorhouse in unprecedented and increasing numbers.

The horror reached a culmination on November 18, when St John, walking home after dark from the distant railway station, was seized by some frightful carnivorous thing and torn to ribbons. His screams had reached the house, and I had hastened to the terrible scene in time to hear a whir of wings and see a vague black cloudy thing silhouetted against the rising moon.

My friend was dying when I spoke to him, and he could not answer coherently. All he could do was to whisper, "The amulet — that damned thing — ."

Then he collapsed, an inert mass of mangled flesh.

I buried him the next midnight in one of our neglected gardens, and mumbled over his body one of the devilish rituals he had loved in life. And as I pronounced the last daemoniac sentence I heard afar on the moor the faint baying of some gigantic hound. The moon was up, but I dared not look at it. And when I saw on the dim lighted moor a wide nebulous shadow sweeping from mound to mound, I shut my eyes and threw myself face down upon the ground. When I arose trembling, I know not how much later, I staggered into the house and made shocking obeisances before the enshrined amulet of green jade.

Being now afraid to live alone in the ancient house on the moor, I departed on the following day for London, taking with me the amulet after destroying by fire and burial the rest of the impious collection in the museum. But after three nights I heard the baying again, and before a week was over felt strange eyes upon me whenever it was dark. One evening as I strolled on Victoria Embankment for some needed air, I saw a black shape obscure one of the reflections of the lamps in the water. A wind stronger than the night-wind rushed by, and I knew that what had befallen St John must soon befall me.

The next day I carefully wrapped the green jade amulet and sailed for Holland. What mercy I might gain by returning the thing to its silent, sleeping owner I knew not; but I felt that I must at least try any step conceivably logical. What the hound was, and why it pursued me, were questions still vague; but I had first heard the baying in that ancient churchyard, and every subsequent event including St John's dying whisper had served to connect the curse with the stealing of the amulet. Accordingly I sank into the nethermost abysses of despair when, at an inn in Rotterdam, I discovered that thieves had despoiled me of this sole means of salvation.

The baying was loud that evening, and in the morning I read of a nameless deed in the vilest quarter of the city. The rabble were in terror, for upon an evil tenement had fallen a red death beyond the foulest previous crime of the neighbourhood. In a squalid thieves' den an entire family had been torn to shreds by an unknown thing which left no trace, and those around had heard all night above the usual clamour of drunken voices a faint, deep, insistent note as of a gigantic hound.

So at last I stood again in that unwholesome churchyard where a pale winter moon cast hideous shadows, and leafless trees drooped sullenly to meet the withered, frosty grass and cracking slabs, and the ivied church pointed a jeering finger at the unfriendly sky, and the night-wind howled maniacally from over frozen swamps and frigid seas. The baying was very faint now, and it ceased altogether as I approached the ancient grave I had once violated, and frightened away an abnormally large horde of bats which had been hovering curiously around it.

I know not why I went thither unless to pray, or gibber out insane pleas and apologies to the calm white thing that lay within; but, whatever my reason, I attacked the half-frozen sod with a desperation partly mine and partly that of a dominating will outside myself. Excavation was much easier than I expected, though at one point I encountered a queer interruption; when a lean vulture darted down out of the cold sky and pecked frantically at the grave-earth until I killed him with a blow of my spade. Finally I reached the rotting oblong box and removed the damp nitrous cover. This is the last rational act I ever performed.

For crouched within that centuried coffin, embraced by a close-packed nightmare retinue of huge, sinewy, sleeping bats, was the bony thing my friend and I had robbed; not clean and placid as we had seen it then, but covered with caked blood and shreds of alien flesh and hair, and leering sentiently at me with phosphorescent sockets and sharp ensanguined fangs yawning twistedly in mockery of my inevitable doom. And when it gave from those grinning jaws a deep, sardonic bay as of some gigantic hound, and I saw that it held in its gory, filthy claw the lost and fateful amulet of green jade, I merely screamed and ran away idiotically, my screams soon dissolving into peals of hysterical laughter.

Madness rides the star-wind... claws and teeth sharpened on centuries of corpses... dripping death astride a Bacchanale of bats from night-black ruins of buried temples of Belial... Now, as the baying of that dead, fleshless monstrosity grows louder and louder, and the stealthy whirring and flapping of those accursed web-wings circles closer and closer, I shall seek with my revolver the oblivion which is my only refuge from the unnamed and unnameable.

The Seal

IWAN GILKIN

Symbol of my fate at hand
A seal with a peculiar gaze
Like a demon come to haunt my days
Inhabits my house most damned.

Inside this cramped and crowded space,
Amidst foot stools and wall hangings,
Scores of trinkets and engravings,
His oval body, his sharp face.

He writhes like a snake sheds its skins
Thrashing round in a monstrous game
While upon his round, flabby frame
He smacks his long, useless fin.

I perceive, with awful fright,
Deep within his sea-green eyes,
Sights of waves grown to huge size,
And squalls like biblical blights.

Frothy valves like ventricles,
The flat scabs of horseshoe crabs,
The seaweed floating green and drab,
Hiding tangles of tentacles.

O Monster, through my eyes now swim
Dreams of dark joy long kept at bay
And the dim image of your prey
Is swallowed by my heart in sin.

Escapee sprung from lowest Dis,
I will now harbour ceaselessly
Torment and love mixed evilly
For this vile, sinister abyss.

But now, before that harsh azure,
And the mire of waves that roll,
I seek, in my reptilian soul,
New worship of truth and grandeur.

Two Cat Poems

CHARLES BAUDELAIRE

Translated by Arthur Symons

LE CHAT

Come on my heart, my amorous cat,
And keep away from me your claws.
Are you more amorous than that
Of metal for agate, passion's pause?
When my hands take on them to caress
Your supple back and splendid head
And with intoxicatedness
My fingers fasten on you with dread,
I see in my spirit my one mistress,
Her eyes like yours, not that nor this tress,
But eyes that penetrate my heart
And her fair feet that make me start
As her brown body in my room
Exhales a dangerous Perfume.

LES CHATS

The wise men love the cats for their perversity,
They love them passionately in their sensual seasons,
Sweet subtle cats, so traitorous in their treasons
That, as they, shiver in their dire adversity.

Lovers of strange science and of sensuality,
They seek the intense horror that makes them furious;
They had been seized as his ghastly slaves by Erebus
Had they inclined to him their sombre savagery.

They assume in dreaming the ancient attitudes
Of the great Sphinxes in the depths of their solitudes
That seem always to sleep in their virginity;
Their pregnant reins are full of the Signs of Magic,
Strange sparks of gold, like fine dust, magically
Shine like stars in their regards, tenebrous, tragic.

The Philosophy of Cats

STANISLAS DE GUAÏTA

No, it is not you that I hate, autumn Wind,
Sad gales, whom I hear sing a monotone hymn,
Between the beams and the floorboards,
Leaves you twist in a slow dance before my eyes,
Nor you, fragile lives breathing their final sighs
Soon to be cut by winter's cords.

Perishing grey Autumn sky, I love you still,
For on this cold day, when the birds cease their trill,
Flames glow in the hearths, shining bright,
And with them return, to homes rural and warm,
Strange cats, their faces of enigmatic form,
And their eyes soft, proud, and alight.

Outdoors, atop the cool grass of the summer
The cats, having played, stretch in sublime slumber,
And, at night, on rooftops high flung,
In the shadows that hide their great lecherous leaps,
Their eyes shine electric, as along they creep,
Meowing loud in their secret tongue.

Beneath the black skeleton of thin, stripped trees,
Heavy with rain, you fall to the ground, dead leaves,
No one ever gave you the chance,
In the yellow brightness of the sun's best beam,
— Dying star, offering up its last alms supreme —
To dance your soft farewell dance!

When it is wet and cold, the cats, female and male,
Enchanters of old, whose steps patter like hale,
As they cross high rooftops of slate,
Crouch next to the hearth, those witches and warlocks.
Their eyes shut tight, awaiting nightfall to stalk,
Arrogantly poised as they wait.

But then, when a sound is unexpectedly heard,
The cat, fast asleep, not a care in the world,
Like a baby in blankets rolled,
The cat, in swift search of what could be amiss,
And, distrustful, shaken from his state of bliss,
Opens his eyes, flecked all with gold.

His green eye, brimming with mischievousness,
Which seems quite troubling for its invasiveness,
Casts a gaze most penetrating:
His stare is clairvoyant and fatalistic,
And therein burns a flame near cabalistic
Which strikes you as captivating.

In your long bodies that your tongues do polish,
O cats, dwells a god who must be acknowledged,
Of clever mind and agile hand,
And when, softly, by the fire, we hear you purr,
One wonders if is hidden beneath your fur,
The soul of Voltaire or Poquelin.

No doubt weary of the banal style of speech,
Of the orators who at social clubs preach,
You choose silence, leaving us stunned.
But you think nonetheless, as human Error,
Drags vain words into great torrents of terror,
And you look on, holding your tongue.

You especially, spoiled by our mistresses,
O cats of the boudoir, objects of kisses,
Caressed by those hands, pale and smart,
In silence, oh! how you must laugh if by chance,
Opening an eye, you were to take a glance,
And read the grimoire of man's heart!

Sredni Vashtar

SAKI

onradin was ten years old, and the doctor had pronounced his professional opinion that the boy would not live another five years. The doctor was silky and effete, and counted for little, but his opinion was endorsed by Mrs de Ropp, who counted for nearly everything. Mrs de Ropp was Conradin's cousin and guardian, and in his eyes she represented those three-fifths of the world that are necessary and disagreeable and real; the other two-fifths, in perpetual antagonism to the foregoing, were summed up in himself and his imagination. One of these days Conradin supposed he would succumb to the mastering pressure of wearisome necessary things—such as illnesses and coddling restrictions and drawn-out dullness. Without his imagination, which was rampant under the spur of loneliness, he would have succumbed long ago.

Mrs de Ropp would never, in her honestest moments, have confessed to herself that she disliked Conradin, though she might have been dimly aware that thwarting him "for his good" was a duty which she did not find particularly irksome. Conradin hated her with a desperate sincerity which he was perfectly able to mask. Such few pleasures as he could contrive for himself gained an added relish from the likelihood that they would be displeasing to his guardian, and from the realm of his imagination she was locked out — an unclean thing, which should find no entrance.

In the dull, cheerless garden, overlooked by so many windows that were ready to open with a message not to do this or that, or a reminder that medicines were due, he found little attraction. The few fruit-trees that it contained were set jealously apart from his plucking, as though they were rare specimens of their kind blooming in an arid waste; it would probably have been difficult to find a market-gardener who would have offered ten shillings for their entire yearly produce. In a forgotten corner, however, almost hidden behind a dismal shrubbery, was a disused tool-shed of respectable proportions, and within its walls Conradin found a haven, something that took on the varying aspects of a playroom and a cathedral. He had peopled it with a legion of familiar phantoms, evoked partly from fragments of history and partly from his own brain, but it also boasted two inmates of flesh and blood. In one corner lived a ragged-plumaged Houdan hen, on which the boy lavished an affection that had scarcely another outlet. Further back in the gloom stood a large hutch, divided into two compartments, one of which was fronted with close iron bars. This was the abode of

a large polecat-ferret, which a friendly butcher-boy had
once smuggled, cage and all, into its present quarters,
in exchange for a long-secreted hoard of small silver.
Conradin was dreadfully afraid of the lithe, sharp-fanged
beast, but it was his most treasured possession. Its very
presence in the tool-shed was a secret and fearful joy, to be
kept scrupulously from the knowledge of the Woman, as
he privately dubbed his cousin. And one day, out of Heaven
knows what material, he spun the beast a wonderful name,
and from that moment it grew into a god and a religion.
The Woman indulged in religion once a week at a church
near by, and took Conradin with her, but to him the church
service was an alien rite in the House of Rimmon. Every
Thursday, in the dim and musty silence of the tool-shed,
he worshipped with mystic and elaborate ceremonial
before the wooden hutch where dwelt Sredni Vashtar, the
great ferret. Red flowers in their season and scarlet berries
in the winter-time were offered at his shrine, for he was a
god who laid some special stress on the fierce impatient
side of things, as opposed to the Woman's religion, which,
as far as Conradin could observe, went to great lengths in
the contrary direction. And on great festivals powdered
nutmeg was strewn in front of his hutch, an important
feature of the offering being that the nutmeg had to be
stolen. These festivals were of irregular occurrence, and
were chiefly appointed to celebrate some passing event.
On one occasion, when Mrs de Ropp suffered from acute
toothache for three days, Conradin kept up the festival
during the entire three days, and almost succeeded in
persuading himself that Sredni Vashtar was personally
responsible for the toothache. If the malady had lasted for
another day the supply of nutmeg would have given out.

The Houdan hen was never drawn into the cult of
Sredni Vashtar. Conradin had long ago settled that she was
an Anabaptist. He did not pretend to have the remotest

knowledge as to what an Anabaptist was, but he privately hoped that it was dashing and not very respectable. Mrs de Ropp was the ground plan on which he based and detested all respectability.

After a while Conradin's absorption in the tool-shed began to attract the notice of his guardian. "It is not good for him to be pottering down there in all weathers," she promptly decided, and at breakfast one morning she announced that the Houdan hen had been sold and taken away overnight. With her short-sighted eyes she peered at Conradin, waiting for an outbreak of rage and sorrow, which she was ready to rebuke with a flow of excellent precepts and reasoning. But Conradin said nothing: there was nothing to be said. Something perhaps in his white set face gave her a momentary qualm, for at tea that afternoon there was toast on the table, a delicacy which she usually banned on the ground that it was bad for him; also because the making of it "gave trouble", a deadly offence in the middle-class feminine eye.

"I thought you liked toast," she exclaimed, with an injured air, observing that he did not touch it.

"Sometimes," said Conradin.

In the shed that evening there was an innovation in the worship of the hutch-god. Conradin had been wont to chant his praises, tonight he asked a boon.

"Do one thing for me, Sredni Vashtar."

The thing was not specified. As Sredni Vashtar was a god he must be supposed to know. And choking back a sob as he looked at that other empty corner, Conradin went back to the world he so hated.

And every night, in the welcome darkness of his bedroom, and every evening in the dusk of the tool-shed, Conradin's bitter litany went up: "Do one thing for me, Sredni Vashtar."

Mrs de Ropp noticed that the visits to the shed did not cease, and one day she made a further journey of inspection.

"What are you keeping in that locked hutch?" she asked. "I believe it's guinea-pigs. I'll have them all cleared away."

Conradin shut his lips tight, but the Woman ransacked his bedroom till she found the carefully hidden key, and forthwith marched down to the shed to complete her discovery. It was a cold afternoon, and Conradin had been bidden to keep to the house. From the furthest window of the dining-room the door of the shed could just be seen beyond the corner of the shrubbery, and there Conradin stationed himself. He saw the Woman enter, and then he imagined her opening the door of the sacred hutch and peering down with her short-sighted eyes into the thick straw bed where his god lay hidden. Perhaps she would prod at the straw in her clumsy impatience. And Conradin fervently breathed his prayer for the last time. But he knew as he prayed that he did not believe. He knew that the Woman would come out presently with that pursed smile he loathed so well on her face, and that in an hour or two the gardener would carry away his wonderful god, a god no longer, but a simple brown ferret in a hutch. And he knew that the Woman would triumph always as she triumphed now, and that he would grow ever more sickly under her pestering and domineering and superior wisdom, till one day nothing would matter much more with him, and the doctor would be proved right. And in the sting and misery of his defeat, he began to chant loudly and defiantly the hymn of his threatened idol:

Sredni Vashtar went forth,
His thoughts were red thoughts and his teeth were white.
His enemies called for peace, but he brought them death.
Sredni Vashtar the Beautiful.

And then of a sudden he stopped his chanting and drew closer to the window-pane. The door of the shed still stood ajar as it had been left, and the minutes were slipping by. They were long minutes, but they slipped by nevertheless. He watched the starlings running and flying in little parties across the lawn; he counted them over and over again, with one eye always on that swinging door. A sour-faced maid came in to lay the table for tea, and still Conradin stood and waited and watched. Hope had crept by inches into his heart, and now a look of triumph began to blaze in his eyes that had only known the wistful patience of defeat. Under his breath, with a furtive exultation, he began once again the paean of victory and devastation. And presently his eyes were rewarded: out through that doorway came a long, low, yellow-and-brown beast, with eyes a-blink at the waning daylight, and dark wet stains around the fur of jaws and throat. Conradin dropped on his knees. The great polecat-ferret made its way down to a small brook at the foot of the garden, drank for a moment, then crossed a little plank bridge and was lost to sight in the bushes. Such was the passing of Sredni Vashtar.

"Tea is ready," said the sour-faced maid; "where is the mistress?"

"She went down to the shed some time ago," said Conradin.

And while the maid went to summon her mistress to tea, Conradin fished a toasting-fork out of the sideboard drawer and proceeded to toast himself a piece of bread. And during the toasting of it and the buttering of it with much butter and the slow enjoyment of eating it, Conradin listened to the noises and silences which fell in quick spasms beyond the dining-room door. The loud foolish screaming of the maid, the answering chorus of wondering ejaculations from the kitchen region, the scuttering footsteps and hurried embassies for outside help, and then, after a lull, the scared sobbings and the shuffling tread of those who bore a heavy burden into the house.

"Whoever will break it to the poor child? I couldn't for the life of me!" exclaimed a shrill voice. And while they debated the matter among themselves, Conradin made himself another piece of toast.

The Rat

HECTOR CHAINAYE

I was sleeping at her side when, suddenly, she woke me with a convulsive movement.

Had she transmitted within me, by the tips of her fingers, the vision of her nightmare? But quickly I see, clearly do I see, a horrible creature sliding upon the curtain of the bed.

"Do you see it? It's a rat!" she cries. "Get it! Get it!"

However, frozen with fear, I am unable to make the slightest movement; and I watch, hypnotized.

The rodent, whose eyes are aglow with a calm, inextinguishable fire, holds its ears still and its back arched, as if it has nothing to fear.

"Kill it!" she cries. "It's biting me! Kill it!"

I was on the verge of striking, when I thought I saw, in the half-light of the alcove, the rat fade away, only to reappear again just as quickly, like a vision.

"Dearest," I then said, taking my lover in my arms, "do not dwell upon your nightmare any further. Think, instead, of our love and our youth. Who does life belong to, if not us?"

When I raised my head, after losing myself within a deep kiss, the rat had disappeared.

Reassured, she fell back asleep.

But I, I kept watch, my brain was troubled, for I know that each apparition has its secret reason for being.

"Tonight," I say to myself, "the mere thought of our youth and our love was enough to drive that dark vision away. But the rat is ever there, watching us. And soon, no doubt, soon in the middle of the night, a night darker than the one spent in this alcove, the rodent will appear again; and then we shall be his."

Bats

JULES RENARD

The night fades, having served its purpose. It does not fade away from its upper stratus, where the stars are found. It fades away like a dress that is dragged upon the ground, between the pebbles and the trees, unto the depths of insalubrious tunnels and fetid caves.

There is not a single corner left untouched by the slivers of night. They are pricked by the thorn, cracked by the cold, spoiled by the mud. And each morning, when the night withdraws, shreds of the dark remain, strewn about haphazardly.

This is how bats are born.

And it is because of this origin that they are unable to bear the brightness of day.

Once the sun has set, as the cool air settles about us, they take flight from old wooden beams where they had hung lethargic, suspended from a claw.

Their clumsy flight troubles us. With a ribbed, featherless wing, they flap about us. They navigate with their ears more than their useless, wounded eyes.

My female companion hides her face, and I turn my head for fear of that impure surprise.

It is said that they would suck our blood to the last drop with more ardour than the love that we feel ourselves.

This is surely an exaggeration!

They are not mean. They never touch us.

Daughters of the night, they hate only the light, and, with a brush of their little funeral shawls, they search for candles that they might extinguish.

BIRDS

Peacocks: A Mood

OLIVE CUSTANCE

In gorgeous plumage, azure, gold and green,
They trample the pale flowers, and their shrill cry
Troubles the garden's bright tranquillity!
Proud birds of Beauty, splendid and serene,
Spreading their brilliant fans, screen after screen
Of burnished sapphire, gemmed with mimic suns —
Strange magic eyes that, so the legend runs,
Will bring misfortune to this fair demesne...

And my gay youth, that, vain and debonair,
Sits in the sunshine — tired at last of play
(A child, that finds the morning all too long),
Tempts with its beauty that disastrous day
When in the gathering darkness of despair
Death shall strike dumb the laughing mouth of song.

Poem IX

GUSTAVE KAHN

Bending low towards the dahlias,
Peacocks ascend the lunar tracing
Branches bow while venerating
Her pale face in the dying dahlias.

She hears from far off brief melodies
Bright night the trees are in tune,
And her tired body is lulled as she swoons
By the sweet rhythm of pure melodies.

The peacocks have raised their ramps of sapphire
For her eyes to descend towards that wearisome hour
    Of things and of sense
Which trails towards the horizon, streaked attire
    Of her body grown dour.
    In her soul hides the flower
Of unnamed desire softened by tales and incense.

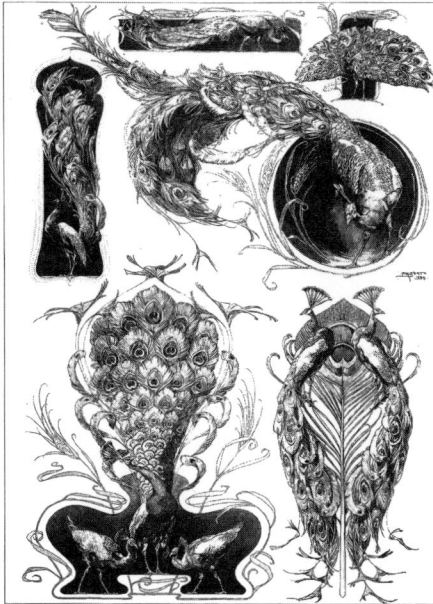

Ennui

MAURICE MAETERLINCK

Indolent peacocks, white peacocks took flight,
White peacocks have fled the dawn's great ennui;
I see white peacocks, peacocks like daylight,
At night I could see peacocks flock to me
Indolent peacocks, peacocks like daylight.
Idly approaching the pond 'neath black trees,
I hear white peacocks, peacocks in their plight,
Idly awaiting the time when light flees.

The White Peacock

WILLIAM SHARP

Here where the sunlight
Floodeth the garden,
Where the pomegranate
Reareth its glory
Of gorgeous blossom;
Where the oleanders
Dream through the noontides
And, like surf o' the sea
Round cliffs of basalt,
The thick magnolias
In billowy masses
Front the sombre green of the ilexes
Here where the heat lies
Pale blue in the hollows,
Where blue are the shadows
On the fronds of the cactus,
Where pale blue the gleaming
Of fir and cypress,
With the cones upon them
Amber or glowing
With virgin gold:

Here where the honey-flower
Makes the heat fragrant,
As though from the gardens
Of Gulistan,
Where the bulbul singeth
Through a mist of roses
A breath were borne:
Here where the dream-flowers,
The cream-white poppies
Silently waver,
And where the Scirocco,
Faint in the hollows,
Foldeth his soft white wings in the sunlight,
And lieth sleeping
Deep in the heart of
A sea of white violets
Here, as the breath, as the soul of this beauty
Moveth in silence, and dreamlike, and slowly,
White as a snow-drift in mountain-valleys
When softly upon it the gold light lingers
White as the foam o' the sea that is driven
O'er billows of azure agleam with sun-yellow:
Cream-white and soft as the breasts of a girl,
Moves the White Peacock, as though through the noontide
A dream of the moonlight were real for a moment.
Dim on the beautiful fan that he spreadeth,
Foldeth and spreadeth abroad in the sunlight,
Dim on the cream-white are blue adumbrations,
Shadows so pale in their delicate blueness
That visions they seem as of vanishing violets,
The fragrant white violets veined with azure,
Pale, pale as the breath of blue smoke in far woodlands.
Here, as the breath, as the soul of this beauty,
White as a cloud through the heats of the noontide
Moves the White Peacock.

The Nightingale and the Rose

OSCAR WILDE

"She said that she would dance with me if I brought her red roses," cried the young Student; "but in all my garden there is no red rose."

From her nest in the holm-oak tree the Nightingale heard him, and she looked out through the leaves, and wondered.

"No red rose in all my garden!" he cried, and his beautiful eyes filled with tears. "Ah, on what little things does happiness depend! I have read all that the wise men have written, and all the secrets of philosophy are mine, yet for want of a red rose is my life made wretched."

"Here at last is a true lover," said the Nightingale. "Night after night have I sung of him, though I knew him not:

night after night have I told his story to the stars, and now I see him. His hair is dark as the hyacinth-blossom, and his lips are red as the rose of his desire; but passion has made his face like pale ivory, and sorrow has set her seal upon his brow."

"The Prince gives a ball to-morrow night," murmured the young Student, "and my love will be of the company. If I bring her a red rose she will dance with me till dawn. If I bring her a red rose, I shall hold her in my arms, and she will lean her head upon my shoulder, and her hand will be clasped in mine. But there is no red rose in my garden, so I shall sit lonely, and she will pass me by. She will have no heed of me, and my heart will break."

"Here indeed is the true lover," said the Nightingale. "What I sing of he suffers: what is joy to me, to him is pain. Surely Love is a wonderful thing. It is more precious than emeralds, and dearer than fine opals. Pearls and pomegranates cannot buy it, nor is it set forth in the market-place. It may not be purchased of the merchants, nor can it be weighed out in the balance for gold."

"The musicians will sit in their gallery," said the young Student, "and play upon their stringed instruments, and my love will dance to the sound of the harp and the violin. She will dance so lightly that her feet will not touch the floor, and the courtiers in their gay dresses will throng round her. But with me she will not dance, for I have no red rose to give her" and he flung himself down on the grass, and buried his face in his hands, and wept.

"Why is he weeping?" asked a little Green Lizard, as he ran past him with his tail in the air.

"Why, indeed?" said a Butterfly, who was fluttering about after a sunbeam.

"Why, indeed?" whispered a Daisy to his neighbour, in a soft, low voice.

"He is weeping for a red rose," said the Nightingale.

"For a red rose!" they cried; "how very ridiculous!" and the little Lizard, who was something of a cynic, laughed outright.

But the Nightingale understood the secret of the Student's sorrow, and she sat silent in the oak-tree, and thought about the mystery of Love.

Suddenly she spread her brown wings for flight, and soared into the air. She passed through the grove like a shadow, and like a shadow she sailed across the garden.

In the centre of the grass-plot was standing a beautiful Rose-tree, and when she saw it, she flew over to it, and lit upon a spray.

"Give me a red rose," she cried, "and I will sing you my sweetest song."

But the Tree shook its head.

"My roses are white," it answered; "as white as the foam of the sea, and whiter than the snow upon the mountain. But go to my brother who grows round the old sun-dial, and perhaps he will give you what you want."

So the Nightingale flew over to the Rose-tree that was growing round the old sun-dial.

"Give me a red rose," she cried, "and I will sing you my sweetest song."

But the Tree shook its head.

"My roses are yellow," it answered; "as yellow as the hair of the mermaiden who sits upon an amber throne, and yellower than the daffodil that blooms in the meadow before the mower comes with his scythe. But go to my brother who grows beneath the Student's window, and perhaps he will give you what you want."

So the Nightingale flew over to the Rose-tree that was growing beneath the Student's window.

"Give me a red rose," she cried, "and I will sing you my sweetest song."

But the Tree shook its head.

"My roses are red," it answered, "as red as the feet of the

dove, and redder than the great fans of coral that wave and wave in the ocean-cavern. But the winter has chilled my veins, and the frost has nipped my buds, and the storm has broken my branches, and I shall have no roses at all this year."

"One red rose is all I want," cried the Nightingale, "only one red rose! Is there no way by which I can get it?"

"There is a way," answered the Tree; "but it is so terrible that I dare not tell it to you."

"Tell it to me," said the Nightingale, "I am not afraid."

"If you want a red rose," said the Tree, "you must build it out of music by moonlight, and stain it with your own heart's-blood. You must sing to me with your breast against a thorn. All night long you must sing to me, and the thorn must pierce your heart, and your life-blood must flow into my veins, and become mine."

"Death is a great price to pay for a red rose," cried the Nightingale, "and Life is very dear to all. It is pleasant to sit in the green wood, and to watch the Sun in his chariot of gold, and the Moon in her chariot of pearl. Sweet is the scent of the hawthorn, and sweet are the bluebells that hide in the valley, and the heather that blows on the hill. Yet Love is better than Life, and what is the heart of a bird compared to the heart of a man?"

So she spread her brown wings for flight, and soared into the air. She swept over the garden like a shadow, and like a shadow she sailed through the grove.

The young Student was still lying on the grass, where she had left him, and the tears were not yet dry in his beautiful eyes.

"Be happy," cried the Nightingale, "be happy; you shall have your red rose. I will build it out of music by moonlight, and stain it with my own heart's-blood. All that I ask of you in return is that you will be a true lover, for Love is wiser than Philosophy, though she is wise, and mightier than

Power, though he is mighty. Flame-coloured are his wings, and coloured like flame is his body. His lips are sweet as honey, and his breath is like frankincense."

The Student looked up from the grass, and listened, but he could not understand what the Nightingale was saying to him, for he only knew the things that are written down in books.

But the Oak-tree understood, and felt sad, for he was very fond of the little Nightingale who had built her nest in his branches.

"Sing me one last song," he whispered; "I shall feel very lonely when you are gone."

So the Nightingale sang to the Oak-tree, and her voice was like water bubbling from a silver jar.

When she had finished her song the Student got up, and pulled a note-book and a lead-pencil out of his pocket.

"She has form," he said to himself, as he walked away through the grove — "that cannot be denied to her; but has she got feeling? I am afraid not. In fact, she is like most artists; she is all style, without any sincerity. She would not sacrifice herself for others. She thinks merely of music, and everybody knows that the arts are selfish. Still, it must be admitted that she has some beautiful notes in her voice. What a pity it is that they do not mean anything, or do any practical good." And he went into his room, and lay down on his little pallet-bed, and began to think of his love; and, after a time, he fell asleep.

And when the Moon shone in the heavens the Nightingale flew to the Rose-tree, and set her breast against the thorn. All night long she sang with her breast against the thorn, and the cold crystal Moon leaned down and listened. All night long she sang, and the thorn went deeper and deeper into her breast, and her life-blood ebbed away from her.

She sang first of the birth of love in the heart of a boy and a girl. And on the topmost spray of the Rose-tree there blossomed a marvellous rose, petal following petal, as song followed song. Pale was it, at first, as the mist that hangs over the river — pale as the feet of the morning, and silver as the wings of the dawn. As the shadow of a rose in a mirror of silver, as the shadow of a rose in a water-pool, so was the rose that blossomed on the topmost spray of the Tree.

But the Tree cried to the Nightingale to press closer against the thorn. "Press closer, little Nightingale," cried the Tree, "or the Day will come before the rose is finished."

So the Nightingale pressed closer against the thorn, and louder and louder grew her song, for she sang of the birth of passion in the soul of a man and a maid.

And a delicate flush of pink came into the leaves of the rose, like the flush in the face of the bridegroom when he kisses the lips of the bride. But the thorn had not yet reached her heart, so the rose's heart remained white, for only a Nightingale's heart's-blood can crimson the heart of a rose.

And the Tree cried to the Nightingale to press closer against the thorn. "Press closer, little Nightingale," cried the Tree, "or the Day will come before the rose is finished."

So the Nightingale pressed closer against the thorn, and the thorn touched her heart, and a fierce pang of pain shot through her. Bitter, bitter was the pain, and wilder and wilder grew her song, for she sang of the Love that is perfected by Death, of the Love that dies not in the tomb.

And the marvellous rose became crimson, like the rose of the eastern sky. Crimson was the girdle of petals, and crimson as a ruby was the heart.

But the Nightingale's voice grew fainter, and her little wings began to beat, and a film came over her eyes. Fainter and fainter grew her song, and she felt something choking her in her throat.

Then she gave one last burst of music. The white Moon heard it, and she forgot the dawn, and lingered on in the sky. The red rose heard it, and it trembled all over with ecstasy, and opened its petals to the cold morning air. Echo bore it to her purple cavern in the hills, and woke the sleeping shepherds from their dreams. It floated through the reeds of the river, and they carried its message to the sea.

"Look, look!" cried the Tree, "the rose is finished now;" but the Nightingale made no answer, for she was lying dead in the long grass, with the thorn in her heart.

And at noon the Student opened his window and looked out.

"Why, what a wonderful piece of luck!" he cried; "here is a red rose! I have never seen any rose like it in all my life. It is so beautiful that I am sure it has a long Latin name;" and he leaned down and plucked it.

Then he put on his hat, and ran up to the Professor's house with the rose in his hand.

The daughter of the Professor was sitting in the doorway winding blue silk on a reel, and her little dog was lying at her feet.

"You said that you would dance with me if I brought you a red rose," cried the Student. "Here is the reddest rose in all the world. You will wear it to-night next your heart, and as we dance together it will tell you how I love you."

But the girl frowned.

"I am afraid it will not go with my dress," she answered; "and, besides, the Chamberlain's nephew has sent me some real jewels, and everybody knows that jewels cost far more than flowers."

"Well, upon my word, you are very ungrateful," said the Student angrily; and he threw the rose into the street, where it fell into the gutter, and a cart-wheel went over it.

"Ungrateful!" said the girl. "I tell you what, you are very rude; and, after all, who are you? Only a Student. Why, I don't believe you have even got silver buckles to your shoes as the Chamberlain's nephew has," and she got up from her chair and went into the house.

"What a silly thing Love is," said the Student as he walked away. "It is not half as useful as Logic, for it does not prove anything, and it is always telling one of things that are not going to happen, and making one believe things that are not true. In fact, it is quite unpractical, and, as in this age to be practical is everything, I shall go back to Philosophy and study Metaphysics."

So he returned to his room and pulled out a great dusty book, and began to read.

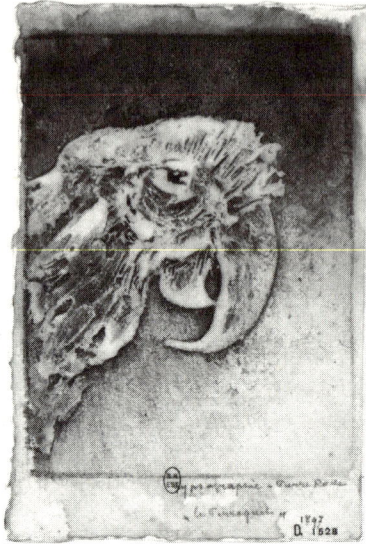

The Parrot, a Dark Tale

CATULLE MENDÈS

For Jean Lorrain

Quite recently, you recalled a tale by the marvellous Banville, the tale with the fateful talking Parrot — a symbol of the House of Ill Repute! In that dreamy yarn, my dear poet, there is a story, a true story, that happened to the pleasant and painful Gérard de Nerval; it was told to us, to Banville, and to myself, by Charles Asselineau, a great friend of Gérard Labrunie; and here it is, less dazzling than the tale, but more faithful to the abominable reality.

C. M.

I

His arms dangling, his head heavy, he had paced, around the table, in the messy bedroom where the two windows, nearly blinded by fog, shone, like a pair of sick eyes, with nothing more than a dim and plaintive gleam, and left the corners to be populated by snatches of furtive shadow that take on shapes, doubtful, troubling, which one would do better not to observe. Just as the half-light cast a rusty gleam upon the copper of the sconces, a tarnish upon the porcelain, dimmed the gold of the cornice on the sideboard, slid slips of crepe over the flowered satin of the chairs, and coated everything in a dust of melancholic mourning, the cowardly languidness of ennui overtook him stealthily, making his mind weak, rendering his heart heavy, discouraging his dreams, irritating his will. Reading, working, he was unable to do either; he had put the volume and the pen to the side, before turning to the second page, without having even written the end of the first verse.

However, on those occasions he found himself unplagued by a bat-like spleen which would drape its limp wings over his temples, Gérard was a young soul, alert and virile, enthusiastic, admirative and creative.

On that day — as is far too often the case, alas! — it plagued him with the hanging weariness of a deflated aerostat. He paced around the table, again, tossing his head heavily. His vitality emasculated, like the failed flight of a dead bird, or like a bow, old and unstrung, trailing upon the ground.

He straightened himself, tossed on a coat, stepped out.

He would go to see Her! The dear young woman, who had always consoled him, reanimated him, exalted him, would soon do so again, with her sister-like softness and her mistress-like tenderness and her Beatrice-like grace that inspired him so, to give him hope, life, and faith, anew. Could anything be morose beneath the smiling gaze of her luminous eyes? Could her breath not resuscitate the kiss upon the cold lips of the dead? Could the gentle tinkling of her voice not awaken his thought, just as the bright cry of the lark is the spark that ignites the morning anew?

She was so pure and so fresh, and, one would say, in full bloom.

When the damp, grey, season comes, the pale, busty little misses leave for the lands of sunshine and goldenness; Gérard did as they did: his heart, sick from the autumn, he went towards the spring.

II

In the street, all was already shadow, before nightfall, an ugly shadow, a grey reflection of a muddy sky, shadows of fog devoid of both the stars and the bright lines of the evening; and the melancholy within him darkened. Although he was impatient to arrive, he walked slowly, with the unsure step of a haggard animal who wanders, lost, not bothering to seek its way. Through the fog that was pierced by a warm rain, he felt himself moistened as if by a slow fever which penetrated him, softened him, rendering him more languid, infusing his very blood with idleness, causing his final resistances to melt into a lukewarm slurry. Beneath his feet, the mud was black, and occasionally there was felt the heavy thickness of some piece of perilously slick refuse. His gaze resolute, he took in this detritus impassively, with a sort of acceptance of his place within a disgusting fraternity; he recognized within it all the lowness and the colour of its fetid inertia; he walked upon it, and he harboured it within himself;

it rose up along his body, entered it, infiltrated his bones, swam within his veins, became his very marrow, his heart, his brain; he believed as well that it seeped from his pores and that it was upon his own self, scattered between the cobblestones that he slid.

He had arrived, at last. It was the door, the dear door. He had only to enter, he did not enter. He stared at it, that door, with a mournful, empty, blank stare; he had, in his degeneration, given up on everything right down to the will to pick himself up, in his loss, down to the desire for salvation. His love of life was dead; and he could not even conceive of the hope of rebirth, so much of what he had possessed as a human had vanished into the humiliating indifference of nothingness. Then, however, because of that supreme cowardice, he was overcome by a disdain of his own self, a nausea rose from his stomach to his lips, and he sensed his mouth fill with a taste so bitter that he felt that he had eaten his own heart. But he did not go in.

A girl passed, heavy and fat, red with blush, stinking of musk, dragging folds of satin and pleats of starch in a noisy shuddering of fabric and mud.

He followed her.

For the taste of refuse triumphs when the ambition of love fails, and Ennui copulates with Evil.

III

When they met, having climbed three flights of stairs and descended a long hallway, in a dark room that must have been an antechamber, he heard the sound of the girl groping along a piece a furniture, searching, no doubt, for the candlestick or the matches; he pressed himself against the closed door, immobile; he was there, and that was all. But a voice began to say, in the shadow:

"Hello, sir, hello! You came, ah! ah! you came, sir. Hello, sir, hello!"

He was frightened, for that voice, which was not, which certainly could not have been that of the girl, resembled greatly the throaty lamentation of someone being strangled. It cried, yelping, tearing, sobbing in a deaf complaint, bursting in a sharp shuddering. It was a voice that one would not have been surprised to hear from the cracked stone of a sepulchre — terrible, gruesome! — But with something grotesque and roguish in its horror: the voice of Pulcinella as the noose tightens around his neck.

The candle was lit. On the highest stick of a perch made of grey wood, leprous for his small white spots, a parrot was flapping his wings and hopping from one foot to another between its two food bowls; an old green parrot, nearly devoid of feathers, whose horrible, scabby neck shrank, stretched, and bobbed — it had but one eye, and this lingering eye opened, round, hard, firm, and troubling like a foreboding omen.

"Be quiet, you filthy beast," said the girl.

"Is that parrot yours?"

"More or less.

"When I rented this flat, I found him in that corner. Some woman must have left him there. I don't know who; no one does. It seems like he's been here for quite some time; he must be sixty years old, at least. Well, he must have heard some real stories, that's for sure! Also, he repeats a bunch of extremely amusing words. Sometimes, it's so funny you could die, I promise you. Would you like to talk to Jacquot?"

"No, thank you."

They went into the bedroom, while the parrot, hopping with fury, his hideous, featherless neck, wildly stretched, and his sole opened even wider, screeched joyously:

"Hello, sir, hello! You came, ah! ah! you came, sir. Hello, sir, hello!"

IV

The hour rang out, he awoke with a start. Where was he? What had happened? He looked around. This room with its red tiles, where abandoned skirts were scattered in billowing heaps, where coloured engravings depicted young girls playing with doves, he was unable to place it, he had, certainly, never seen it. Ah! a dream, no doubt. A raspy breath, right next to him, snored. He leapt as he withheld a cry of horror! And he remembered: it was disgusting, and it was true. He had come here, him! He whose soul was delighted by dreams and whose heart was ecstatic with love, he had wallowed, voluntarily, in that bestiality and in that crapulence. Beautiful and exquisite, and so pure, and eternally loving, she was waiting for him, the dear young woman, and he had abandoned her to follow — oh! that girl. His lips upon which there flourished the memory of a pink kiss, had been sullied by that mouth that stank of Bully vinegar, absinthe, and lethargy. Monstrous, monstrous abjection of souls in the clutches of the Demon Spleen!

Dazed, he contemplated himself in the mirror, hoping that he would be unable to recognize himself. It was him, it was him! Running towards the mirror, he spat in the face of his reflection. And, now, a great disgust came over him, nauseating waves rose within his throat. Oh! If only he could have vomited his infamy, as one might a disgusting wine consumed the night before. He came, went, with shivers, stopping himself, his head between his hands, his chest heaving and his heart leaping convulsively, and suddenly he spread his hands, his sullied hands. A desire gripped him, wild, absurd, and it would not leave him, to plunge himself in cold water, frozen, where he would be washed of that creature, of that room, and of that hideous sofa, and of himself.

But, at least, not one minute more, not one second more, would he stay in that abominable place.

He threw some money onto the bed — while the young girl continued to sleep, a deep sleep like that of a placid beast — and headed towards the door, and fled, was there no more.

In the antechamber, he stopped, stunned.

Someone had spoken! Surely, someone had spoken! Who, though? The girl? No, she was snoring. But then, who? And what had they said? He had not been able to make it out. The voice started again, a sinister voice that seemed to whine and laugh at the same time:

"Goodbye, sir, goodbye! You will be back. Ah! ah! you will be back, sir! Goodbye, sir, goodbye."

He remembered, threw himself into the hallway, plugging his ears.

But the strident voice of the parrot followed him, unflagging:

"You will be back, ah! ah! sir, you will be back!"

The Owls

CHARLES BAUDELAIRE

Translated by Arthur Symons

Under the yew-tree's heavy weight
The owls stand in their sullen fashions,
Like Pagan gods of Pagan passions
They dart their eyes and meditate.
Unmoving they stare with living flame
Until the end of the melancholy
Hour sees the oblique sun set in folly
And darkness falls in shades of shame.
Their aspect to the wise man teaches
All that he needs, all he beseeches,
Tumult and change and discontent;
The man drunk of a shadow that passes
Keeps always the imperishable scent
That makes the wind change and the grasses.

Sunset Wings

D. G. ROSSETTI

To-night this sunset spreads two golden wings
Cleaving the western sky;
Winged too with wind it is, and winnowings
Of birds; as if the day's last hour in rings
Of strenuous flight must die.
Sun-steeped in fire, the homeward pinions sway
Above the dovecote-tops;
And clouds of starlings, ere they rest with day,
Sink, clamorous like mill-water, at wild play,
By turns in every copse:
Each tree heart-deep the wrangling rout receives, —
Save for the whirr within,
You could not tell the starlings from the leaves;
Then one great puff of wings, and the swarm heaves
Away with all its din.

'L'Oiseau Bleu': A Painting on Silk by Charles Conder

MAX BEERBOHM

O ver them, ever over them, floats the Blue Bird; and they, the *ennuyées* and the *ennuyants*, the *ennuyantes* and the *ennuyés*, these Parisians of 1830, are lolling in a charmed, charming circle, whilst two of their order, the young Duc de Belhabit et Profil-Perdu with the girl to whom he has but recently been married, move hither or thither vaguely, their faces upturned, making vain efforts to lure down the elusive creature. The haze of very early morning pervades the garden which is the scene of their faint aspiration. One cannot see very clearly there. The ladies' furbelows are blurred against the foliage, and the lilac-bushes loom through the air as though they were white clouds full of rain. One cannot see the ladies' faces very clearly. One guesses them, though, to be supercilious and smiling, all with the curved lips and the raised eyebrows of Experience. For, in their time, all these ladies, and all their lovers with them, have tried to catch this same Blue Bird, and have been full of hope that it would come fluttering down to them at last. Now they are tired of trying, knowing that to try were foolish and of no avail. Yet it is pleasant for them to see, as here, others intent on the old pastime. Perhaps — who knows? — some day the bird will be trapped... Ah, look! Monsieur Le Duc almost touched its wing! Well for him, after all, that he did not more than that! Had he caught it and caged it, and hung the gilt cage in the boudoir of Madame la Duchesse, doubtless the bird would have turned out to be but a moping, drooping, moulting creature, with not a song to its little throat; doubtless the blue colour is but dye, and would soon have faded from wings and breast. And see! Madame la Duchesse looks a shade fatigued. She must not exert herself too much. Also, the magic hour is all but over. Soon there will be sunbeams to dispel the dawn's vapour; and the Blue Bird, with the sun sparkling on its wings, will have soared away out of sight. *Allons!* The little rogue is still at large.

The Egg of the Albatross

ERIC STENBOCK

The top of a disused lighthouse, surrounded by the sea, hardly seems to be a convenient or desirable residence for a little girl: This was the residence of Marina.

The people of Varenha did not seem to think there was anything very extraordinary about it. She had always been there: and when her father and mother died, they left her there all alone. Besides, there was something uncanny about her; and although she was a familiar figure in the town, and in fact rather a pet, at the same time people thought it just as well that she should live a little way off.

Varenha is an island in the West Indies not much known to the general public; but, nevertheless, many foreigners alight there in search of rare orchids and butterflies, and particularly of the eggs of waterfowl, who have there one of their greatest fastnesses. Such foreigners as do come thither are mostly wealthy people, and have yachts of their own, and on them the island thrives. It is only every now and then that a steamer touches there.

When I say Marina's father and mother died in the lighthouse I am not strictly accurate, because they were not her father and mother: and she, instead of being found under the traditional gooseberry bush, was hauled up in a mackerel net at the early age of three. Where she came from, and what she was, nobody ever knew. When she was picked up she could not speak at all. She was not drowned: on the contrary, she was swimming about quite naturally, as a puppy or kitten might do. According to the best authorities, she had the peculiar fairness and other characteristics of the Octoroon. But people generally regarded her as something not of this world. She did not seem to understand or respond to any known language; but she soon learnt to talk Portuguese. The old people, whose only child had been drowned years ago, became devoted to this strange sea-baby, whom they called Marina, from her origin.

A new lighthouse had been built, but they were allowed to keep their old quarters. The two old people died almost simultaneously; so leaving Marina alone. She belonged to no one, and nobody particularly wished to take charge of her. But, as I have said before, she was rather a favourite in the town, when she appeared on market-days with her curious wares; for this is how she made her living.

She would gather all manner of curious and iridescent shells and make them into necklaces, or boxes, and such like things. Likewise she made curious bouquets of dried seaweeds. But her chief source of income were the eggs of the gulls, guillemots, sea-swallows, penguins, and the like.

Strange to say, all these wild creatures were perfectly tame to her. They would come to her to be fed, and actually allowed her to take their eggs from their nest. She never took more than one from each nest. She was singularly nimble of foot, and would climb up to their fastnesses.

In this trade she had a speciality. If any one else had attempted to take their eggs, the assembled waterfowl of all kinds would unanimously and unmercifully have attacked them.

So, once a week, the quaint little figure could be seen crossing in her little boat, which she had painted green herself, encrusted with corals and shells in strange devices.

She was very simply clad in one single loose white garment, bound rather curiously with a sea-green sash made of silk; on one exceptionally lucky day she had found means to purchase this one article of finery, which had always attracted her fancy. She was always barefooted; but she wore shell necklaces and bracelets, and also wore wreaths in her hair of delicate seaweeds.

Her eyes were green; her hair a peculiar nuance, which also in certain lights looked green. So it was not very wonderful for the superstitious people to think her a water-sprite.

So, though living all alone and unprotected, she was quite safe, as no one would dare to rob or molest her. She spent the rest of her time in swimming and rowing about, or running along the rocks in search of various sea-products. Perhaps on these occasions her toilet was less complete than it was on Saturdays.

I am afraid poor Marina was a heathen. Again, what is everybody's business is nobody's business. It was nobody's business to give her religious instruction, or indeed any instruction whatever. The priests in that part are not of a very high order; generally even more superstitious than their flocks. The worthy Padre did not care to come much in contact with the creature he thought not quite human; and besides, there was no one to pay him for instructing her. Indeed some people averred she had never even been baptized.

One day some vague sense of religion did wake in her; she saw in a shop-window an intaglio, in some green stone, representing a venerable-looking old man with a trident, standing between two long tumbled lines of sea, from which emerged beautiful figures of maidens with long streaming hair, and beautiful youths playing on spiral shell-trumpets. This pleased her immensely. So much so that she determined to purchase it at the cost of all her savings, which, I think, amounted to three dollars. So one day she went to the shop, and triumphantly demanded the article, displaying what she supposed to be her vast wealth.

"But, my dear," said the shopman, "the price of that is fifty dollars."

She stood aghast. Fifty dollars! She had never heard of so much money in her life.

Then she began to cry silently.

There happened to be an intellectual-looking Englishman in the shop, who had come to the island in his yacht in search of orchids. He was struck both with the pathos and the humour of the situation. He paid down the fifty dollars, and gave the intaglio to the child.

She could not believe her senses; and disappeared like a flash of lightning, clutching her treasure to her bosom; ran at full speed through the town, jumped into her boat and rowed quickly across, and did not rest till she had reached her airy nest in safety.

She had occasionally wandered into the church, and got a few confused notions of a cult which she did not understand; so, by way of imitation, she hung up the intaglio in the corner of the room, and placed a perpetual light to burn before it.

I may here fitly describe what the room was like. It was hexagonal; she had painted it herself with a curious wavy pattern in her favourite sea-green. But all the corners she had encrusted with shells and seaweed; of which she also had fashioned an elaborate frieze. The furniture was very simple indeed: the only table was utilised to support a large aquarium, which also was a present from a rich foreigner; and that she had arranged with a kind of fairy garden, with seaweeds for trees, and all manner of beautiful sea anemones for flowers. The rest of the furniture consisted of two large boxes: in one box she had made herself a luxurious bed with the shed feathers of the wild sea-birds; in the other box there was something still more extraordinary at the moment this story commences, namely, an albatross sitting upon her egg. There was no chair; for if she sat down at all, she sat on the floor; also no fireplace, as in Varenha it is never cold. And she spent most of her time in the open air; and as she found her food on the sea-shore, she had no need of cooking. Indeed, so self-supporting was she, that she would first make a meal on a mollusc, and then sell the shell.

On exceptional occasions she would treat herself to a seaweed salad, which is by no means so unpalatable as it sounds to those who have never tasted one.

The windows were always open, and the wild sea-birds would fly out and in; she used to buy food for them in the town, which cost her much more than her own food ever did.

But her chief friend was an albatross, whom she called Almotâna, who had made her nest for three successive years in her box. Indeed, when the albatross flew out, Marina would sit on the nest and keep the egg warm herself; which the albatross understood, as she never flew away unless the little girl was there. Once a day during the season another bigger albatross, whom she called Wandafra, would come to visit his wife. But he did not see the fun of sitting on the egg if the little girl would undertake that office for him. How she came to choose these names, which conformed to no known language, is difficult to ascertain. All that is known is that when she was first picked up she gabbled some unintelligible jargon, which ever afterwards she had been heard to murmur to herself.

One day a steamer *did* land at Varenha. It was quasi-private, and more or less going round the world. There were all sorts and conditions of people in it; or rather, I mean, many sorts, but one condition: e.g. there were collectors, who wished to land at Varenha to collect various objects which were their particular hobby, and sportsmen who thought it great fun to shoot guillemots; but no steerage passengers.

Among these was a certain German professor, called Sammler. Herr Sammler collected everything. From being a poor professor of zoology and botany, he had unexpectedly come into a considerable fortune. So now he was enabled to indulge his mania to the full.

One Saturday, as usual, Marina went with her wares to the marketplace; it was just at the beginning of the breeding season, and she had an unusually good collection of various eggs.

There came up to her stall a benevolent-looking old gentleman with a long white beard and a pair of spectacles, accompanied by a well-known character in the town, a certain Portuguese Jew, called Levi Mendès, who used to act as guide and interpreter to foreigners who landed at the island. The benevolent-looking gentleman took a great interest in Marina's eggs. His knowledge of Portuguese was somewhat limited; so he had to converse chiefly by means of the interpreter. There seemed to be some dispute between them — in German, a language which of course Marina could not understand. But her quick intelligence divined that the Jew wished to beat down her prices, whereas the German was willing to give her more than she asked. It ended by Herr Sammler — for this was he — giving her more money than she had ever got before. Then Mendès drew Professor Sammler aside, and this was their conversation: —

"You said you particularly wanted to get an albatross egg, Herr Professor. Now that little girl has one. You know they are rather difficult to get."

"I know that," said the Professor. "Besides, in this island there is a peculiar variety of albatross. It would be indeed something if I could get one of their eggs."

"Well," said the Jew, "I think I could get it for you — and cheap too. The child does not know the value of money. If you will pardon me saying so, I think it was injudicious of you to give her so much for those other eggs. And of course she has no notion of comparative value."

"I certainly should not think of taking advantage of a little girl," said the Professor. "I will give her a fair price for it. But let us go back, and you can arrange for me to see the egg."

They came back again to her stall. The Jew said insinuatingly —

"This great Senhor is particularly desirous of seeing your albatross egg. Would you mind showing it to him?"

"Oh no," said Marina, who was impressed by the benevolent appearance of the stranger, and only too proud of showing off her treasures.

"What time could we most conveniently come?" asked Mendès.

"Oh, to-morrow afternoon at three," said the little girl. "Then our Almotâna goes out for her afternoon fly."

So next day Herr Sammler and his guide presented themselves at the lighthouse, where they found Marina sitting as usual on the egg.

"Isn't it beautiful?" she said, rising and pointing the egg out to the Professor.

"May the Senhor look at it?" asked Levi.

"I don't know whether Almotâna would like it," said Marina; "but if he is very careful with it —"

The Professor took the egg up in his hand.

Strange is the mania for collecting. People who would otherwise be incapable of a dishonest action resort even to theft in order to obtain some rare object which they especially covet.

"Tell her," said Herr Sammler, "I will give her twenty dollars for it."

"The Senhor says he will give you two dollars for it," says Mendès.

"No, no, no! you must give it me back," cried Marina.

"No, my dear," blurted out the German, in very broken Portuguese, "not two dollars, but twenty dollars — twenty-five dollars!"

"No, this is not to be sold," cried the little girl. "Almotâna only lays one egg, and what will she say if she finds her egg gone?"

She began to cry bitterly. But the Professor, under the influence of the lust of collection, calmly put the egg in his pocket, but, being naturally of a kindly nature, tried to soothe the child, and produced from his pocket two bank-notes of twenty dollars each.

Marina had never seen a bank-note before. She took the paper, not knowing in the least what it meant.

"You'd better come away," said Mendès; and hurried Herr Sammler down the stairs.

The child, clutching the bank-notes in her hand, followed them; and her little boat managed to overtake their large boat with four rowers. Then she followed them through the town, saying in piteous monotony —

"Give me back my egg!"

Of course a crowd of people gathered together, and naturally asked what all the fuss was about.

"I do not know what she means," said Mendès. "She is mad. See, the Senhor has bought her albatross egg. Here is the egg. And he has given her forty dollars for it. See, she has the forty dollars in her hand."

And so she had — two crumpled notes, almost crushed to pieces by the sculls of her boat.

The people tried to explain that the Señor had bought it.

"It is his, and he has given you a very, very great deal of money for it."

Suddenly Marina attempted to seize the egg from Mendès; and in the scuffle the egg fell to the ground and was smashed.

Marina turned deadly pale, and fell down in a dead faint.

The German, whom I have said before was a kindly man, caused her to be taken to his hotel, and instructed his landlady to put her into the best bed she could find.

The landlady, who was a good kind of woman, and likewise because she wished to oblige the Professor, and feared to do any ill to the water-sprite, treated her with the utmost gentleness.

Marina remained for a long time unconscious, and then reviving to semi-consciousness, fell asleep. Seeing her in a natural sleep the landlady left her. But she did not wake till dawn.

She found herself in a huge room and a large bed. It was some time before she could realise and recollect. Then, clad only in a night-gown as she was, she opened the window, and managed somehow to slide down the water-pipe, and escaped.

When she got to her fastness again, she called out "Almotâna! Almotâna!" telling as best she could in her strange jargon to the bird what had happened.

There was no answer, but a long wail. She caught sight of the albatross circling round and round, lamenting the loss of her only egg. She went to the window and stretched out her arms and implored Almotâna to come in. But she only continued circling round and wailing.

At last, in her attempts to catch the albatross, she overbalanced herself, and fell straight into the water.

Of course the fall was fatal.

A strange thing was to be seen that morning on the seashore: the body of a child in a simple white night-gown washed ashore; standing over it, with wings outspread, an albatross. Just then a boat came in sight — one of the boats from the steamer. In it were two Englishmen. One of them was a thick-set and aggressively muscular young man, of that peculiarly English type; well-formed, perhaps, but wholly without grace; healthy, perhaps, but wholly without bloom, or the expression of vitality, those stupid, dull, apathetic, impudent eyes, peculiar to this breed; features perhaps well formed, but utterly dull and stolid, without any charm of expression; with a thick, coarse, abundant growth of hair. He was clad in a sort of knickerbocker suit of a loud check pattern, a stick-up collar, and a cap; he carried a gun in his hand.

The other was of a different type: an older man, with something intellectual and refined about his features.

"I say, Jenkins," said the young man, "here is a chance: there's an albatross. We shall be able to get one after all. You remember the devil of a fuss we had with that one we hooked: and the bloody brute went and broke the hook, and went off with it."

"I thought that was horrible!" said the other man. "The bird was quite tame, and followed the ship for days. Remember the fate of the Ancient Mariner."

"Damn the Ancient Mariner!" said the other.

"No, I didn't suppose you were familiar with the story of the Ancient Mariner. But there is another consideration of a more practical kind that I wish to urge upon you. You had better not shoot the albatross, because the people here have a kind of superstitious regard for them, and you might get into a great row if you did."

"What do I care what these damned bloody Portuguese think?" said the young man, taking aim. He shot. And the shot went home.

And at that moment a much larger albatross swooped down, and hit him one terrible blow with his powerful wing. And his companion had little difficulty in ascertaining that he had been killed at once.

Stranger still was the sight that met the eyes of the fisherfolk as they went down to the sea to ply their usual avocation. There was Marina lying dead: and on her bosom the dead albatross, shot through the heart. And circling round, in circles sometimes wide and sometimes narrow, a male albatross, bewailing the death of his mate.

Ballad of the Bird-Bride

ROSAMUND MARRIOTT WATSON

They never come back, though I loved them well;
I watch the South in vain;
The snow-bound skies are blear and grey,
Waste and wide is the wild gull's way,
And she comes never again.

Years agone, on the flat white strand,
I won my sweet sea-girl:
Wrapped in my coat of the snow-white fur,
I watched the wild birds settle and stir,
The grey gulls gather and whirl.

One, the greatest of all the flock,
Perched on an ice-floe bare,
Called and cried as her heart were broke,
And straight they were changed, that fleet bird-folk,
To women young and fair.

Swift I sprang from my hiding-place
And held the fairest fast;
I held her fast, the sweet, strange thing:
Her comrades skirled, but they all took wing,
And smote me as they passed.

I bore her safe to my warm snow house;
Full sweetly there she smiled;
And yet, whenever the shrill winds blew,
She would beat her long white arms anew,
And her eyes glanced quick and wild.

But I took her to wife, and clothed her warm
With skins of the gleaming seal;
Her wandering glances sank to rest
When she held a babe to her fair, warm breast,
And she loved me dear and leal.

Together we tracked the fox and the seal,
And at her behest I swore
That bird and beast my bow might slay
For meat and for raiment, day by day,
But never a grey gull more.

A weariful watch I keep for aye
'Mid the snow and the changeless frost:
Woe is me for my broken word!
Woe, woe's me for my bonny bird,
My bird and the love-time lost!

Have ye forgotten the old keen life?
The hut with the skin-strewn floor?
O winged white wife, and children three,
Is there no room left in your hearts for me,
Or our home on the low sea-shore?

Once the quarry was scarce and shy,
Sharp hunger gnawed us sore,
My spoken oath was clean forgot,
My bow twanged thrice with a swift, straight shot,
And slew me sea-gulls four.

The sun hung red on the sky's dull breast,
The snow was wet and red;
Her voice shrilled out in a woeful cry,
She beat her long white arms on high,
"The hour is here," she said.

She beat her arms, and she cried full fain
As she swayed and wavered there.
"Fetch me the feathers, my children three,
Feathers and plumes for you and me,
Bonny grey wings to wear!"

They ran to her side, our children three,
With the plumage black and grey;
Then she bent her down and drew them near,
She laid the plumes on our children dear,
'Mid the snow and the salt sea-spray.

"Babes of mine, of the wild wind's kin,
Feather ye quick, nor stay.
Oh, oho! but the wild winds blow!
Babes of mine, it is time to go:
Up, dear hearts, and away!"

And lo! the grey plumes covered them all,
Shoulder and breast and brow.
I felt the wind of their whirling flight:
Was it sea or sky? was it day or night?
It is always night-time now.

Dear, will you never relent, come back?
I loved you long and true.
O winged white wife, and our children three,
Of the wild wind's kin though ye surely be,
Are ye not of my kin too?

Ay, ye once were mine, and, till I forget,
Ye are mine forever and aye,
Mine, wherever your wild wings go,
While shrill winds whistle across the snow
And the skies are blear and grey.

Upon the Threshold

REMY DE GOURMONT

t the Château de la Fourche, all was grand and sad: that name, which is sinister at first glance, is a memory of the harsh, primitive, seignorial justices; the four sombre avenues whose lamentations made a sound like the ocean; the moat, where black storks swam amidst broken reeds, the menacing hemlocks and so many yellow flowers in bloom, but like deadly suns; the castle, with its walls the colour of a stormy sky, its roof sunken with grooves like a ploughed field, its narrow ogive windows with their trefoils, its uncrowned tower, prey to a formidable ivy which seemed like the very perpetuity of life itself.

The steps climbed and the doorway passed, one entered into a series of vast rooms, high and cold, furnished with oak, lined with greeneries that mimicked the bending reeds of the moat, its mournful flowers and its hemlocks, sheltering within their frozen shadow the royal promenade of disillusioned storks. No rug other than the mats of straw; dogs sleeping everywhere, noses between their paws, and, strange spectre (to which I never grew accustomed), drifting from room to room, clacking its beak as soon as the doors were opened, a domesticated heron. This mournful being went everywhere; he followed us at mealtime, pecking at his food in a bowl that we set out for him, making, at regular intervals, a noise like that of a tile upon an old wall being shaken by the wind. We called him the Missionary, because he seemed, with his slanting, paternal gaze, to be like a reverent Capuchin Father who had preached during a mission at la Fourche — and whose death, which came several days after, had coincided with the apparition of the bird, wounded by a gunshot and found in the moat by the gamekeeper.

This story, a bit ridiculous, had amused me, on the first night I spent at la Fourche, when my host told it to me in a tone which, however, precluded any sort of joviality; but, from that next day on, the Missionary had frightened me, less with his ugliness than with his confidence, with the certitude by which that animal seemed to be in his own home, to be its master, and, truly, to be accomplishing a supernatural mission within it. Never did we chase him out, never did we lock him in; as soon as his beak rapped against a door, one of us rose to open it for him, and, if he left at the same time as us, he went out first, solemn and with the appearance of, not just any Capuchin, but the appearance of an aged judge, incorruptible and sweetly merciless.

The Missionary: internally, I had given him another name, Remorse.

However, one night as we left the table, having dined on venison and juniper-flavoured cider, I bumped into the bird near the door and, hurriedly, beneath my breath I said:

"Well, go already, Remorse!"

"Why don't you call him the Missionary?" the Marquis de la Hogue asked me rudely, seizing my arm and looking at me with eyes alight with a feeling which I first took to be rage, but which was terror.

Then, with a voice that trembled and cracked at each word, as if it sought, despite itself, to extract the secret:

"How do you know that he is named Remorse? Who told you?"

"You!"

And by this singular word uttered at random, for I was almost as troubled as M. de la Hogue, I had secured for myself future confidences.

When we entered into the room where our evening chats were to take place, the bird was in front of the fireplace, where trees were aflame, standing upon one leg, its beak beneath its wing. Wishing to resume our dialogue, I said simply, as I sat in one of the wooden armchairs, which resembled cathedral stalls:

"Is he asleep?"

"He never sleeps!" responded M. de la Hogue — and, indeed, as a brighter gleam leapt from the hearth, I saw, cold and ironic, fixed upon me with the dirty glow of a star seen reflected in a frog pond, the eye of the old judge, an eye which was incorruptible and sweetly merciless.

"He never sleeps," M. de la Hogue resumed; "nor do I. My heart never sleeps. I know sleep, I do not know unconsciousness. My dreams are very much the continuation of my evening thoughts, and, in the morning, for the past thirty years, I reconnect my dreams so logically to my thoughts, that I do not remember having ceased my swim in full intellectual clarity for even an hour. And of what do I dream during these interminable hours of my life? Of nothing, or rather, of negations, of what I did not do, of what I will not do, of what I would not do, even if youth were restored to me. For, this is how I am, I am he who has never acted, never raised a finger in the name of accomplishing a desire or a duty. I am that lake whose surface the wind has never wrinkled, that forest which remains unrustled, that sky untroubled by clouds of action."

He fell silent for several seconds, after those sentences which were slightly solemn — declamatory, even. Then:

"Do you know my life? No, you are too young, and anyway what the world knows of me is not me. I have never told of myself, and, without the chance event — or the providential perspicacity — that earlier made you utter a word — a name! — which haunted me (I will admit), you would not receive tonight, you neither, my confession.

Here it is:

I was eight years old, when my mother brought home for me from a distant voyage a little girl who was more or less my age, our cousin, at least by name, and the death of whose parents had left her as dangerously alone in the world as a little lamb lost in the middle of the woods at night. That adorable young girl was immediately spoiled, and, for me, an ideal younger sister, or perhaps even an obvious fiancée, an angel fallen from the stars for my eternal consolation. At twelve years, with my heart precocious and vigorous, a boy having grown up among the pastures, I already adored Nigelle with an infinite love which, consequently, until the day that I lost her, could neither grow nor shrink. She loved me as well, with an identical ardour; I knew it, and the confession that she, dying, made to me, taught me nothing about my own wickedness.

From the moment that a bit of reasoning was possible within my boyish brain, I made of life a conception which was singular, and, I feel it now, criminal, too. Having cut a rose, one afternoon as its exasperated perfume tempted me and the purple of her smile birthed within me a desire for conquest, having wandered in the alleys of the garden with my rose cut and forgotten between my fingers, I saw in less than an hour that it had withered and was now sad, wounded by the arrows of the sun — and I thought that one must desire roses, but one must not cut them.

And I thought as well, as Nigelle moved in front of me, that one must desire women, but one must not cut them.

Many thoughts assailed me at the moment of that primordial discovery and, slowly, the whole philosophy of the void, a whole nirvanic religion developed within my feeble, prideful head. One day, I resumed it for myself in the following, simple, way:

One must remain upon the threshold.

Several books had helped me, ascetic writings, a summary of Plato, condensed versions of German metaphysical works, but, practically speaking, my doctrine was entirely my own. I became quite proud of it and I plunged myself resolutely into the shadows of inaction.

I endeavoured to commit only the simplest acts and especially those which, not promising me any sort of exceptional pleasure, could not cause me any disappointment.

I had violent desires, I wallowed in them, I rolled in them, I gorged myself upon them. My heart became so swollen that it could have contained the world. Desiring everything, I had everything, but I did not have everything in the same way that one can hold within their hands two other trembling hands. I took everything, but nothing gave itself to me; I had everything — but without love!

It was only later, in a solemn moment, that I knew the existence of love. Until that moment, pride had given me the illusion of it, and I lived perfectly happily, proud to escape the disenchantment born of each accomplished act.

Today even, and now that I know, now that pain has taught me, it would be impossible for me to cut the rose. What good would it do? That horrible refrain sings ceaselessly within my head and it has never been more imperative.

Nigelle and I lived alongside one another for twenty years: she, becoming shyer and sadder with each day, alarmed at my fortune, the poor woman who possessed nothing beyond the ripe harvest of her blond hair; myself, increasingly prideful and indestructibly mute.

I loved her as much as one can love, but I did not love her unto the threshold.

I have never crossed this threshold — not even my shadow has, and not even the shadow of my heart has ventured into that palace of love.

Hospitable and tender, the door was always open, but I turned my head as I passed by, to contemplate my own desire, to speak with my desire, to confide unto my desire the dreams that I wanted to leave unrealized.

Crossing the threshold? And after? That palace was perhaps a palace like any other palace — but the palace of my dreams was unique and such that one will never see the likes of it again.

She died for loving me, who loved her with a love which I will once again qualify as infinite. She died saying to me: 'I love you!' And myself, I could manage nothing in response."

The heron changed legs, snapped its beak, sliding it from beneath the left wing, to beneath the right: its mournful, ironic, eye was not watching M. de la Hogue.

"That bird", resumed my host, "strikes you as quite ugly and absurd, does it not?"

"Quite dour, especially."

"Absurd and dour. I bear him like a punishment. He scares me, he causes me to suffer, and I want it to be so. You can well understand that, if I desired to wring his neck, it would be no sooner said than done!"

"Have you thought of that?" I said, "Wringing Remorse's neck?"

"I have thought of it," responded M. de la Hogue. "But, what good would it do? There is no meaning in this absurd, dour, animal, beyond the one that my will gives it; I have only to deny him for him to become as dead as a stuffed bird. Do you think that that I am oblivious to its inanity? Do you take me for a madman?"

The old man had risen, shaking his long grey hair that wept down his pale, hollow, cheeks; then, suddenly calmed, he let himself collapse once more into his chair.

Entirely calm and somewhat sardonic, he repeated himself:

"I suppose that you take me for a madman?"

Because I was smiling as I watched him, and mechanically stretching my hand out towards the feathers of the immobile bird, he rose again:

"Do not touch the Missionary!"

He had said these words with a voice which must have been that of Charles I saying to an onlooker upon the scaffold: "Do not touch the axe!"

The Swan Killer

VILLIERS DE L'ISLE-ADAM

"Les cygnes comprennent les signes."
[Swans understand the signs.]
Victor Hugo. *Les Misérables*.[1]

For M. Jean Marras

aving scoured volume upon volume of Natural History texts, our illustrious friend, the doctor Tribulat Bonhomet came to learn that *"the swan does in fact sing before it dies."* — Indeed (he recently admitted to us once more), it was this music alone, since he had heard it, that helped him bear the disappointments of life and any other seemed to him to be nothing more than *charivari*, than "Wagner."

— But how had he come to experience this joy for the first time? — This is how:

In the area around the old, fortified city where he lives, that practical old specimen had, one fine day, discovered within an abandoned secular park, beneath the shadows of great trees, an old sacred pond — upon the fissured mirror of which were gliding twelve or fifteen tranquil birds — and carefully studied the surroundings, meditated upon the distances, noticing especially the black swan, their watchman who was sleeping, lost in a ray of sunlight.

Each night, that swan held watch with his great eyes open wide, a polished stone within his long pink beak, and, were he to detect the smallest threat to those whom he guarded, he would, with a movement of his neck, abruptly cast into the wave, into the middle of the white circle of his sleeping fellows, the awakening stone: — and, at that signal, the troupe, still guided by him, would fly away through the darkness beneath the dark pathways, toward some distant stretch of grass, or some fountain reflecting grey statues, or some other asylum well-fixed within their memory. — And Bonhomet had considered them for a long while, in silence — smiling at them, even. Was it not with their final song that he dreamt of soon filling his ears, as would a perfect dilatant?

Sometimes, then — as midnight rang out over some moonless, autumnal night — Bonhomet, in the grips of insomnia, would rise suddenly, and, for the occasion of the concert that he needed to hear once more, dress specially. The gigantic and bony doctor, having stuffed his legs into a pair of oversized rubber boots, which extended, seamlessly, out from a long, ample raincoat, dutifully stuffed as well, would slide his hands into a pair of stainless steel gloves, originally from a Medieval suit of armour, (the gloves of which he became the happy purchaser of for the fine price of thirty-eight sols — a steal! — in an antique shop). That done, he would fix his wide, modern hat, blow out his lamp, descend his staircase, and, once the key to his residence had been placed within his pocket, set off, in bourgeoise fashion, to the edge of the abandoned park.

Soon, he was boldly making his way across dark pathways, towards the retreat of his favourite singers — towards the pond whose water, which was shallow and well-plumbed in all places, did not exceed the height of his waist. And, beneath the archways of leaves that surrounded the shores, he muffled his steps, mindful to avoid the dead branches.

Upon reaching the edge of the pond, it was slowly, so slowly — and without so much as a sound! — that he would chance one boot, and then another — and move forward, through the water, with unprecedented precaution, so unprecedented that he scarcely dared to breathe. Like an opera-lover before the anticipated cavatina. He moved in such a way that, in order to take the twenty steps that separated him from his dear virtuosos, he would generally spend between two and two and a half hours, such was the level of care that he took to not disturb their black watchman.

The breath of the starless skies rustled the highest branches in the shadows around the pond plaintively: — but Bonhomet, without allowing himself to be distracted by the mysterious murmur, crept forward imperceptibly, and so well that, around three o'clock in the morning, he would find himself, invisible, a half-step away from the black swan, without him detecting the slightest hint as to his presence.

Then, the good doctor, smiling in the shadows, would scratch, softly, so softly, scarcely graze, with the tip of his index finger from the Middle Ages, the ruined surface of the water, before the watchman!... And he would scratch with such a gentleness that the swan, although surprised, did not judge the importance of that vague alarm worthy of throwing the stone. He listened. At length, his instinct, slowly taking in the *idea* of danger, his heart, oh! his poor ingenious heart would begin to beat horribly: — and it filled Bonhomet with jubilation.

And so it was that the beautiful swans, one after the other, troubled, by that sound, from the depth of their slumber, would undulantly unfold their heads from under their pale silver wings, — and, beneath the weight of Bonhomet's shadow, enter gradually into a state of anxiety, having who knows what kind of confused understanding of the mortal peril threatening them. But, in their infinite delicateness, they suffered in silence, like the watchman, — not being able to fly, *because the stone was not thrown!* And every heart of those white *exilés* began to pound in deafening agony — *intelligible* and distinct for the delighted ear of the excellent doctor who — knowing full well as he did, what his mere proximity was causing, *morally*, to them — delighting, in incomparable pruritus, in the terrific sensation that his immobility was inflicting upon them.

"How sweet it is to encourage the artists!" he whispered to himself softly.

For three-quarters of an hour, approximately, he experienced an ecstasy that he would not have swapped for a whole kingdom. Suddenly, the rays of the Morning Star, sliding through the branches, would illuminate, in an improvisational way, Bonhomet, the dark water, and the swans with their dream-filled eyes! The watchman, stricken with horror by that sight, would throw the stone... — Too late!... Bonhomet, with a horrible cry, beneath which his syrupy smile seemed to unmask itself, would leap forward, claws raised, arms outstretched, across the rows of sacred birds! And swift was the grasp of this modern knight's iron fingers: and the pure, snowy necks of two or three singers would be slit or snapped before the radiant flight of the other poet-birds.

Then, the soul of the dying birds would exhale, unheeding of the good doctor, in a song of immortal hope, deliverance, and love, towards unknown Skies.

The rational doctor would then smile at that sentimentality, of which he dared savour, as a serious connoisseur, but one thing—THE TIMBRE.Musically, he sought only the singular softness of the timbre of those symbolic voices, which vocalized Death as if it were a melody.

His eyes closed, Bonhomet would inhale, into his heart, those harmonious vibrations: then, wobbling, as if gripped by seizure, would go to collapse upon the bank, stretching out upon the grass, lying down upon his back, in his warm and waterproof clothing.

And there, that Patron of our era, lost in a voluptuous torpor, would savour anew, in the depths of his being, the memory of that delicious song — even though it was tinged with a sublimeness which he found outmoded — sung by his dear artists.

And, resorbing his comatose ecstasy, he would ruminate, in bourgeoise fashion, upon that exquisite impression until the sun rose.

ENDNOTES

1   It is needless (we feel) to add that in this authentic quotation, it is not the Author of *The Mouth of Shadow* who is speaking, — but — simply *one of his characters*. It would be rather unfair, then, to attribute to an Author *even* the blasphemous courtroom monstrosities or vile turns of phrase that, for personal and perhaps noble reasons — he resigns himself, sadly, to placing in the mouths of certain Ilotes of his imagination. [Note from Villiers.]

The virgin, vivacious, and lovely day at hand...

STÉPHANE MALLARMÉ

The virgin, vivacious, and lovely day at hand
Will it rend for us with a blow of its wild wing
This hard lake left haunted beneath the frost's cold sting
By the pure, clear ice of flights frozen where they stand!

A swan from before recalls that this is the land
That he must flee, a glorious but forlorn king
For forgetting of which place he was meant to sing
When from the sparse, sterile winter the ennui ran.

Shaking his great neck, across space he will disband
That white agony, denying gravity's demand
Save when his plumage is caught, horror of the land.

A phantom banished for his shine like the dawn,
He pauses to think of the scorn to withstand
During the long, useless exile of the Swan.

Wild Swans at Coole

W. B. YEATS

The trees are in their autumn beauty,
The woodland paths are dry,
Under the October twilight the water
Mirrors a still sky;
Upon the brimming water among the stones
Are nine-and-fifty swans.

The nineteenth autumn has come upon me
Since I first made my count;
I saw, before I had well finished,
All suddenly mount
And scatter wheeling in great broken rings
Upon their clamorous wings.

I have looked upon those brilliant creatures,
And now my heart is sore.
All's changed since I, hearing at twilight,
The first time on this shore,
The bell-beat of their wings above my head,
Trod with a lighter tread.

Unwearied still, lover by lover,
They paddle in the cold
Companionable streams or climb the air;
Their hearts have not grown old;
Passion or conquest, wander where they will,
Attend upon them still.

But now they drift on the still water,
Mysterious, beautiful;
Among what rushes will they build,
By what lake's edge or pool
Delight men's eyes when I awake some day
To find they have flown away?

FISH & HERPTILES

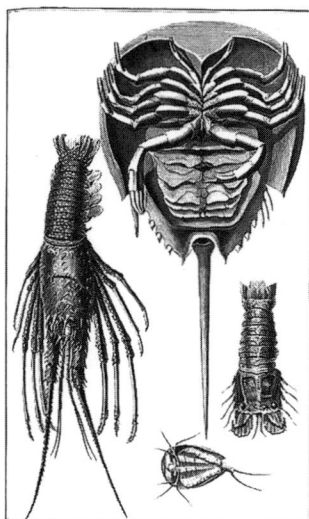

The Berlin Aquarium

JORIS-KARL HUYSMANS

I do not think that there exists a city uglier or more fastidious than Berlin, which seems to have been cut into sections with a ruler, and planted with pointless houses and horrible palaces. Its Spree is a joke of dirty water, its Brandenburg Gate a junky pastiche of the Athenian Propylaia, its famous Unter den Linden is even more mediocre than our Champs-Élysées, and its Friedrichstrasse, its Willelmstrasse, its Leipzigerstrasse — all of its luxurious avenues — cannot even equal the low opulence of our high streets.

And so, the city is hideous and one wishes that the crowd dwelling there were less so; but, they too, are cause for consternation. Upon the sidewalks stroll greasy officers stuffed into tight fitting tunics and black trousers with red thread; and they pass, upright, a monocle as big as the wheel of a locomotive over one eye, chewing, in torrents of smoke, tree trunks and bouncing, upon the cobblestones, sabres; and then there are, squeezed into suits whose tones offend, fat women with mouths that are perpetually open and from which escape, every so often, bursts of laughter like the cries of a hen, and men, broad-backed, with golden glasses, bald heads, patchy beards, ruddy cheeks, and faces like those of homeopathic pharmacists and university intellectuals. Here one can observe aspects of human ugliness which are particularly insolent in the case of the officer, silly in the case of the woman, and, dire in the case of the bourgeois man.

The desire to board a train and to flee harangues you, then you tell yourself that you are being unfair, that, after all, Berlin harbours a magnificent museum of old paintings and an aquarium which is absolutely extraordinary, a fairyland of wild flowers, such as few cities possess.

This aquarium is housed within cellars which have been converted into spacious grottos. One hears only the dim rumbling of the cars racing above and cries from the macaws that salute you upon entering; and one has the impression that, though it is noontime, one has been transported to the evening, into a zoological garden illuminated by gaslight; in the windows, one can see rolled cables that are snakes, then crocodiles in shallow pools and birds in cages, finally a seedy, burlesque bar where the patrons are seated within the skeleton of a whale and appear to be in a prison, when seen from the other side of the carcass, as if they were behind curved, white, bars. But all of this is nothing more than twaddle spouted by naturalists and trinkets that shine in the doorway. The true spectacle stretches the length of a gallery whose partitions are walls of water, held in place by frames of glass; and a bright, underwater, daylight bathes the interior of the porthole windows, illuminating with its greenish glints cliffs built for the Myrmidons and forests for pygmies; and no terrestrial vegetation can match the delicacy of these small trees, the lightness of these branches. The flora of the sea grows in these small rocks and in baskets of lace flowers and of guipure plants, embroidered with a needle, elaborate like Alençon veils. The clumps of seaweed sprawl across these miniscule prairies, tangled together within their wild lashes, their tethers of scarlet velvet, their straps of green leather, linking transparent liana groves with pearly red trunks and pink leaves.

And fish race above, fish with ferocious eyes and funny appearances, some bulging like wineskins, others slender like the blade of a knife; some are hunchbacked, and others are equipped with crescent-shaped fins and a mouth that yawns in the middle of their bellies, and they are covered in scales set in a semi-circular pattern like the tiles on a rooftop, like the tracery on a coat of mail, with links of gold and silver, incrusted with shining jewels and set with gems; they rush, veering with a sudden flick of their tale when they find themselves face to face, and darting their heads downwards, sliding beneath the bushes of red coral, grazing the thickets of the reefs, pushing, as they pass, the fields of that strange sponge that is called Neptune's Glove and resembles an open hand of wool whose fingers wave in the air.

Can there be found, amongst these species whose scientific names are impossible to pronounce, a specimen of that fabulous fish who, according to the older authors, grazes, in the Southern Seas, upon the plants of coral, just as the sheep graze upon the herbs of the field in the countryside? I do not know; but, as particular as these fish

may be, they belong at least to a well-defined genus, to a
special family of natural history, to groups of individuals
who are living and known; they cannot be confused with
animals of another race; thus their strangeness is merely
relative and, furthermore, all the big aquariums have
fish of this kind; the zoological glory of Berlin is not to be
found there; rather it can be found in the nearby boxes,
in the individual compartments of seawater where there
dwell beings which are both beasts and flowers; hybrid
beings, improbable, and nevertheless real; and they swarm,
sparking analogies of the most extravagant sort, images
of the most baroque variety; the wildest of orchids seem
reasonable next to them and there is not to be found
anywhere on earth a butterfly or bird whose shine can be
compared to theirs.

It is the garden of the Mermaids and the menagerie of
the Undines.

On a site bristling with jagged rocks, one remarks,
through the green fog of the waters, Bryozoa, foam animals,
some domed like clumps of peacock-blue velvet, others
drifting like tufts of unkempt wool: these here are like a
film of boiling lead; those there are like the cream on the
surface of milk turned green or the froth of a stew whose
greyness is tinted with silver; and these foams which
softly wave vibrating lashes and fine hair are graced with
a mouth, an oesophagus, a gizzard, and a stomach; they
snap up smaller animals, savouring the infusoria, feasting
ceaselessly upon an imperceptible prey, loving, perhaps,
and in any case, reproducing. Then, living wisely in their
midst, the marvel of the seas, the anemone that live upon
the surface of the rocks or in their scattered fragments. In
them one finds confirmed the unlikelihood of tones and
the folly of forms. The most well-behaved of them look a bit
like the anemones of our gardens and certain sorts of cacti;
but the others!

One of these zoophytes, the Caryophyllia, is a woman's corset in white satin, garnished with a hive of batiste on the upper half; and this corset closes upon just one breast, but is placed, pointing upwards, in the direction of the neck; and this point, which is the tender green of a young sprout, emerges from a pale, snow-coloured nipple, surrounded almost from its birth by an entirely new scarf of cherry fluff.

And there are other flowers around it too, sporting as well the most deceptive tones and the wildest contours: wigs of fire supported by patera of bronze; wax the colour of capuchins whose locks are tousled by blue-green barbels; swifts with hilts of jade and ropes speckled with a dew of blood; then there are stems like sticks of sprouted cinnamon, with, at their peaks, great daisies whose hearts sparkle like carbuncles in rays of gold; shafts, half-bright and half-milky, burst at their summit like the radiant disc of a monstrance; and the host is pink and the creases of the Holy Sacrament are mauve; others still, with increasingly incoherent aspects, stretch spider webs of emerald green, wherein are sewn, in place of dead flies, pearls; others resemble the luminous core of a cabbage, puffs of rice powder, badgers with white beards, with orange fur, mounted upon sleeves of a bright vermillion, others, at last, are the crimson hays of mad artichokes!

And these flowers walk and these beasts take root; they commandeer worms, aquatic larvae, newly-hatched fish, swallow them, and, as would a good drunk, when they have gorged themselves too greatly, vomit. Add to that that these anemones secrete corrosive, venomous, juice, and that they sting and burn like nettles once they are touched.

And the encased beaches continue to stretch on, in the rooms of the aquarium, and defiant acts of zoology parade before the spectator. After the Bryozoa and the corallites, appear the annelids, wormlike florae, caterpillar plants with metallic reflections, worms whose bodies are a series of short, puffy rings of silk which grow like the ridges on a hunting knife when rubbed; one of them is red, crossed with a line of ink upon its back and it has black lips and blue eyes; another, the giant bristle worm of the West-Indies, possesses a coat of enamel with a red trunk and its rings, which are rainbow-coloured, are studded with spikes; this creature is ferocious and devours even its own kind; another animal, quite extraordinary as well, is the Holothurian, a great lilac cucumber whose head is a white daisy. Its specificity is that it spews its viscera when bothered, which also causes its death.

To summarize this stroll across the world of the seas, they say that God seems to have saved his most extravagant beasts for the mysterious depths of his gulfs. He fused, in an inexplicable amalgam, the flora of the earth and the fauna cultivated in walking gardens and blooming menageries; then, in order to further outdo his own work, he used the gleam of the mineral realm, animated the stones and transported within the adornments of his creatures the fire of his gemstones.

Then, in an absolute contrast, while he let us see the magnificent animals of his lands, he placed us as well in the presence of abominable creatures, monsters such that nothing but the delirium of maladies could have birthed; and there, he no longer summoned the aid of his stones and his plants, but seemed to borrow the contours and the colours of the metals forged by man in his factories.

And the making of this decision reveals itself in the maritime museum of Berlin, where, behind the glass partitions, a nightmarish creature stirs, a metallic monster, a sort of crab armed like a warship, the Limulus Polyphemus of America, I believe.

Imagine a beast buried beneath a piece of grey sheet metal, with raised edges that seem to have been sculpted with a hammer and painted with minium, a crustacean with the vague shape of a torpedo boat and evoking with its armour the image of an American monitor whose visible propellor is a long tail. The head is hidden and, when one looks closely, one can see two small eyes lying in wait behind loopholes, then two dewlaps that hang like anchor chains. When at rest beneath the water, this being can lose itself within the tone of the sand; but, when it moves, it is another thing altogether; it then becomes quite simply atrocious. I saw it, one day, turned over, swimming upon its back and nothing can communicate the horror of that body like a bellows, of that black, folded flesh, playing like an accordion in the waves, and of those purple legs streaked with white. And those ten legs seemed like twenty, seemed like one hundred, for they moved so quickly; then the beast put itself back into place and let itself collapse; and its shell flattened, like a felt hat, as it sank into a crevasse wherein it disappeared, between two rocks.

That crustacean that one would think—were it not alive—fabricated in the factories of Krupp or in the forges of Le Creusot does not belie the notion that it was, like the others, created by the Lord of Genesis; despite its ultra-modern appearance, it could only have been invented during the age of the false gods, by one of the demons of paganism; indeed, one recalls that those beings copulated to bring forth monsters and this explains, in turn, the filiation of that crab. It must have been engendered on a pile of rubbish and born of the works of Phobetor, the god of frightening dreams, and of Forina, the sordid goddess of the sewers.

In any case, his image follows, when, having left the aquarium, one has climbed back up to the street, into broad daylight; and then, it has to be said, the ugliness of the Berliners seems gentle and one would almost like, my word, to kiss them, so attractive they now seem, the faces of the monocle-clad sword-draggers and the homeopaths with their glasses of gold.

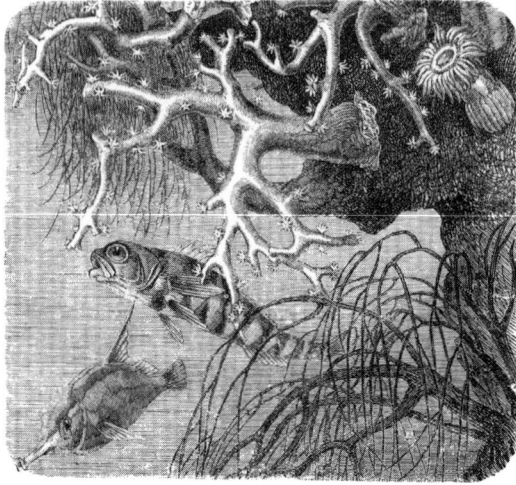

The Aquarium

JULES LAFORGUE

To Gustave Kahn

D o you know the land where Silence blooms? The entrance fee is but a franc — cheaper, but also less frequented, than the Opera — and two sous for the coat check, for outside it is raining, but here it is piously and obligingly warm.

A labyrinth like a network of caves, with ominous gaslights in the vaulted ceilings, corridors diverging to the left and the right of the luminous glass of the underwater compartments — it's the Aquarium swirling about in its humdrum cave, interrupted, solely, from time to time, by the piston of the hydraulic machine — it's the Aquarium where one takes part in the most unspoiled underworld, in interior scenes the furthest removed from the worlds we know — silence! like in the bedroom of an infirmary, the honourable company, one day we shall see the Aquarium raised to the rank of an institution of public good.

Moors of dolmens incrusted with viscous jewels — circuses of basaltic steps where crabs (who are very much at home — please understand!) of an obtuse and hesitating humour, an after-dinner-sort of good mood, tumble and tangle in pairs, with jesting little eyes of a deadpan disposition;

— Oh! that high-plateau where, suspended from its suckers, an octopus holds Vigil, flabby, floating minotaur of the realm!...

And then plains of fine sand, so fine that they are sometimes stirred by the wind from the flat tail of a passing fish as he arrives from afar in a floating oriflamme of liberty! His passage watched by large desert rose eyes, here and there, his coming enough to fill the day's paper...

Straddled by natural bridges, parades of ponderous horseshoe crabs with slatey shells and tails like rats; several of them overturned upon their backs and struggling, but perhaps they did it themselves to give their backs a scratch? We will never know (and as for me, would I be so out of place, upon my back, among those crabs?)...

And fields of sponges, sponges like a detritus of lungs, cultures of truffles in orange velvet, and a whole cemetery of pearly-orange molluscs, and precious plantations of asparagus, tumefied and preserved in the alcohol of Silence...

And the desolation of steppes inhabited by a lone tree, lightning-struck and ossified, an occasional phalanstery where clusters of seahorses unpretentiously make their colonies...

And beneath chaotic, abandoned arcs of triumph, sea needles twist like frolicsome ribbons...

And I shall show you all the underwater areas!

Eggs hang, lain by I know not what, and for how long? Like string beans at the ends of twisting threads...

And the whirlwind migrations of unkempt nuclei, lashes in a tuft round an eye that is to be fanned during the ennui of long voyages...

And those wells far to the wayside, gynoecium more wayward still, laboratories of experiments even more mysterious, where, floating in ascensions, oh!, they climb only to be ripped asunder! Bubbles that are perhaps pregnant, bubbles of bluish gelatine contracted in a perpetual and identical diaphanous spasm...

And so on and so forth.

But at last, and as far as the eye can see, prairies, prairies dappled with white anemones, fat, pointed onions, bulbs with purple mucus, bits of tripe erring here and there, and my faith reconstituting its very existence, stumps whose antennae wink at the coral across the way, a thousand warts seemingly devoid of purpose; — a whole cloistral, foetal flora, vibratorily stirring the eternal digestive dream of being able to whisper mutual congratulations on the state of these things back and forth to one another...

Oh! I know what you are going to say to me, dear friends who flatten their noses now against those windows! Yes, how easily one imagines oneself in their place! Neither day, nor night, nor autumn, nor winter, nor springtime, nor summer, and no other such changes; only dream in the very droppings of the cradle, and love without changing places, cool within this unflappable blindness — just cool!

It's closing time! It's closing time! And climbing back up, returning to the brightness of day and all the muddiness, frivolousness, fiacrousness, boorishness, crookedness, catarrhoustuousness, dubiousness, and aggressiveness of 1886!

Oh, but before they close, you are in the underwater realm yet, and we are drying out, parched by a supra-terrestrial thirst; this is the difference that I wish to point out. And why do the antennae of our senses, our very own, why are they not restricted by Silence and Opacity and Blindness? Can they sense the flair of what is beyond possible for us? And do they ever pump endlessly upon a well long since dry? And do we know how to wedge ourselves into our own little corner to sleep off the bender brought on by our own little egos? — This is what I wished to say, as we leave *this world of satisfied creatures*.

Now, oh underwater vacationers, I find no difficulty in admitting that we have, in our above-ground cravings, two fruits that are perhaps worthy of yours: the face of a beloved who, exhausted, has shut their eyes and fallen asleep upon pale pillows, coils of their hair wet and sticky from the day's final sweat, and their mouth open and wounded, showing their pale teeth in the light of an aquarium beam from the Moon (oh! do not disturb it! do not disturb it!), and the Moon itself, that sunflower, flattened, dried, from agnosticism...

But the beloved is so close, and the Moon so far! At least, at certain hours. Anyway, what of those certain times? Instead of always, always, being "time?" — Dialogue: What time is it, I ask you, passer-by? — *It is Time, go, it is Time;* — (and how I wish that might also mean: Oh! You need not hurry!)

Oh! To have even to set these things down in writing, these things that an aedileship, wizened and prudent, should take upon themselves!

Snake-charm

JOHN TODHUNTER

Into this dusky bower
Of sylvan quiet,
Where roses and rank vines
Only run riot,
Whence comest thou, dark Shape, at this sweet hour,
Into this lonely bower?

"I am the spectral form
Of hopes forgotten,
Birth-strangled babes of joy
Left to grow rotten,
Corpses of unborn deeds, devoured still warm
By sloth's corrupting swarm."

Welcome, thou dismal guest,
Sit down beside me,
Lie by me all night long,
Sting me and chide me.
At dawn I'll gather fruits to lull thy rest,
Thou serpent of the breast!

A Tortoise

MICHAEL FIELD

χελώνη

There is laughter soft and free
'Neath the pines of Thessaly,
Thrilling echoes, thrilling cries
Of pursuit, delight, surprise;
Dryope beneath the trees
With the Hamadryades
Plays upon the mountain-side:
Now they meet, and now they hide.

On the hot and sandy ground,
Crumbling still as still they bound,
Crouches, basks a tortoise; all
But the mortal maiden fall
Back in trepidation; she
Takes the creature on her knee,
Strokes the ardent shell, and lays
Even her cheek against its blaze,

'Till she calms her playmates' fear;
Suddenly beside her ear
Flashes forth a tongue; the beast
Changes, and with shape released
Grows into a serpent bright,
Covetous, subduing, tight
Round her body backward bent
In forlorn astonishment.

With their convoluted strain
His upreaching coils attain
Full ascendancy — her breast
By their passion is compressed
'Till her breath in terror fails;
Mid the flicker on the scales,
Half she seems to hear, half sees,
How each frighted comrade flees.

And alone beneath the pine,
With the serpent's heavy twine
On her form, she almost dies:
But a magic from his eyes
Keeps her living, and entranced
At the wonder that has chanced,
As she feels a god within
Fiery looks that thrill and win.

'Tis Apollo in disguise
Holds possession of his prize.
Thus he binds in fetters dire
Those for whom he knows desire;
Mortal loves or poets — all
He must dominate, enthrall
By the rapture of his sway,
Which shall either bless or slay.

So she shudders with a joy
Which no childish fears alloy,
For the spell is round her now
Which has made old prophets bow
Tremulous and wild. An hour
Must she glow beneath his power,
Then a dryad shy and strange
Through the firs thereafter range.

For she joins the troop of those
Dedicate to joy and woes,
Whom by stricture of his love
Leto's son has raised above
Other mortals, who, endowed
With existence unallowed
To their fellows, wander free,
Girt with earth's own mystery.

To My Tortoise Chronos

EUGENE LEE-HAMILTON

Thou vague dumb crawler with the groping head
As listless to the sun as to the showers,
Thou very image of the wingless Hours
Now creeping past me with their feet of lead:
For thee and me the same small garden bed
Is the whole world: the same half life is ours;
And year by year, as Fate restricts my powers,
I grow more like thee, and the soul grows dead.
No, Tortoise: from thy like in days of old
Was made the living lyre; and mighty strings
Spanned thy green shell with pure vibrating gold.
The notes soared up, on strong but trembling wings,
Through ether's lower zones; then, growing bold,
Spurned earth for ever and its wingless things.

The Frog Killer

RACHILDE

To Eugène Demolder.

mall, light, poised in the night upon his pale sheet like a water insect on the surface of a clear pond, the boy listens. A finger woke him, he thinks, a wet finger, grazing his forehead.

It's not God's finger, because God is now too old to take care of his children. Silence has replaced him. God is now a cripple no longer able to gallop upon the wind, and he sent the wind to its stable where it can sometimes be heard snorting behind the gate.

Vast silence, with its cold index finger, woke the boy who now listens, stunned, finding that which he is unable to hear quite dark.

Posed upon four legs, his many slender limbs rigid like stalks of wheat, his thighs long, his hocks strong, his fine feet — those of one designed to jump — flatten, his eyes look all about, his head lowered slyly, his hair falling like a heavy rain, streaking his temples with lines darker than the night, and beneath his hair his resolute pupils shine, like two veiled lights, for this young boy, stripped bare, appears to be in a state of mourning.

He lives like an animal, coming, going, eating, sleeping, without saying a word. He possesses only the corner of the bedroom, a filthy corner, next to the wood-burner. He lives there like a cricket. In the winter he keeps warm next to the cinders. In the summer, air comes to him through a hole in the roof near the chimney. His bed is a screen of reeds lashed firmly to old chair legs. On top of it, a mat of heather and a sheet were dispassionately thrown by someone... he's had the same for a year now. Well taught, the little boy shakes out this sheet every morning while his mother boils their soup, because he noticed that lice don't like flames, and all the vermin burn or drown in the pot.

But, on this June night, it is not the lice that woke him. He sensed someone walking, silently, about him. The wind has perhaps escaped God's stable? Or maybe there is a weasel? Or maybe a rat, one of those big field rats, brown, furry, with a smooth tail, like a snake? No, no one...

And the boy advances a bit on his palms, upon his knees, lowers his head further, raising his rump. In a single leap, if necessary, he will be up and on his feet in the middle of the room; he needs only to uncoil his legs, like a spring, to find his footing. He knows that at night things do not move as they do during the day. During the day animals do as they please, but at night they do as they must, and when the birds have closed their eyes, other unknown animals take flight and travel in great bounds, grazing the ground. He knows this and other things still, this little boy of ten years that they allow to hang listlessly about the house, returning only to sleep and eat poor food that often causes his lips to bleed.

Nothing is heard; only, near the fence made of brooms that surrounds the garden — cabbages, beets, and a lovely onion — *the earth screamed!* The earth has a way of crying that is truly *terrible*. She is mute and only ever makes the sound of grinding teeth. If someone, man or beast, performs a forbidden deed, she attempts to sound the alarm, and, more faithful than a good dog, she does not spoil their deeds with needless cries; a rolling pebble, crunching sand, the imperceptible sound of a snail shell being crushed, are enough for her.

And someone somewhere is always grinding the tiny little bones of death, for the earth is filled with them. And the tiny little bones of death always protest.

Someone was certainly moving near the vegetable patch. A thief? There for the onions, no doubt. Little Toniot rose with his habitual leap, springing up like an insect or a toad, nude from his head to his toes, his member and his ears extended. He had the idea to wake his father, big Toniot, who was sleeping in their second bedroom, beneath the hunting rifle that was hung on the wall, big Toniot, so tired from his most recent watch.

But was it necessary to awaken such a tired man, who had ended up going to bed alone, uninterested in so much talking?

Little Toniot did not think of his mother, because, for him, man of ten, women did not count. He despised them. His mother would beat him, and he would laugh, silently, after her, because women spread their fingers before they hit you, and only strike your face with a gust of wind; it makes a slapping sound and hardly hurts; while men, men hit with a closed fist; big Toniot would hit very hard like that, and he had a lot of respect for his father, because, amongst other reasons, he was the owner of a real hunting rifle.

Decidedly, it was the thief who was coming his way, the onion thief. Little Toniot could not have been more sure of it. The tiny bones of death were protesting. Damp all over with the sweat of a bad night's sleep, the slender body of the boy was hunched over a worm-riddled chest where they packed the bread and the lard — the two treasures of that house. He had the appearance of a wet little cat watching a big rat, despite the fact that he was frozen, and his carnivore instinct was stirring within him the sour desire to track his prey. If it revealed itself to be much bigger than him, he would make sure to quietly call upon big Toniot... like the ground complains when we press upon it.

From his corner, little Toniot could not see anything. The room had no window beyond the door and the hole by the chimney. By day, sunlight entered through the door. The moon saved the hole by the chimney for certain nights, when it would pass its white hands through the opening, through the soot, caressing the kettle that hung and causing it to sparkle like silver. That moon always woke little Toniot, who would *hear it shine*. Ah! why didn't it enter while his teeth were chattering, while he was there frightened in the edge of his chest? The light is so nice. And now, as if by a miracle, it was opening the door, the door that was always locked from the inside. Yes, it was indeed the moon, as a real person, a beautiful woman who appeared quite pale for the darkness of the night, a woman who was fully nude, full-figured, her hips full and plump such as it becomes a living star, her throat high and firm, her whole face veiled by red hair.

Toniot had never feared animals, nor females, but he was terrified of this moon who was now before him dressed as a woman. Mechanically, he made the motion to sweep his hair away from his forehead, the forehead of a stubborn child, and he saw, with inexpressible horror, this gesture reflected upon the forehead of the moon as if he were looking at his own reflection in a mirror.

—What's it? What're yeh doing there, yeh little toad? You ain't asleep at this hour?

The woman, face to face with her young son, began scolding him relentlessly.

—I ain't doing nothing, he responded, resting his cheek upon his raised elbow.

—Why're you up then, you little beast? Why're you weaslin' about? And yer father, where's he? Did'ya wake yer dad, you little wretch?

—No, I woke m'self because I'd 'erd a crackin' in the garden.

—And that'll be the first time that there's crackin' in the garden, won't it, you little pig? At night, there's cracking everywhere! D'ye need to catch the sounds all by the tail, you little weasel?

—I thought it was coming from the onions! It was like the foot of a man!...

—The foot of a man? Little shit!

And before little Toniot had thought of lifting his elbow, the woman seized him violently by the shoulder and pushed him towards his bed of heather, in the corner of their sty where he should have stayed until it was time to wake. There, mutely, blindly, she struck the boy with her fists closed tight, gripped by a wrathful rage despite the fact that he had committed no trespass.

Absolutely naked, the child received the blows in the correct places, silently, in the way he had become disdainfully accustomed to, and, that night, it seemed to him that he would be killed if he were to complain in even the slightest way.

The mother seemed drunk.

—I'll tie you up, vermin, she repeated to herself softly,

clenching her fists and her teeth even further, I'll tie you up by your paws, like a chicken in the market!

And so he responded, in an equally low voice, understanding that he had to give himself over, obeying an order sent from a place higher than the blows being struck:

—And what? You're mad? Why ain't you got a shirt on tonight? Get it over with or you're going to wake him.

The woman stopped suddenly, and threw her hair back behind her.

Little Toniot imitated her.

They looked at one another from the depths of the shadows where the heaving flanks of the mother were casting a strange sort of glow. And each was ashamed of their sad nakedness.

Crouched upon his sheet, patting his poor limbs which would be blue by morning, the boy considered the female with a look of suffering curiosity, protecting his little member with his left hand, because he knew that if she hit him again there, it would be over for the *little toad*, who would go croak and then die.

Ah, that, why had she suddenly decided to start hitting like a man? Can naked women do whatever they want? What mystery had entered into the room with the clarity of pale skin? He shivered in fright.

—Ah, I'm more tired'n if I'd hanged ya, little worm! The mother murmured, turning her back on him to slip on her nightgown.

It was as if the moon had finally left their house. All grew dark and Toniot breathed freely.

Big Toniot was thin, dirty. He had the sad appearance of an ensnared wolf, the kind who would chew off his own foot for lack of a better alternative. His grey cloth pants, which had taken on a greenish aspect from spending too much time rubbing against the moss of the forest and the grass of the hills, slid pathetically upon his spindly hips, revealing, between his belt and his little patched jacket, an impressive strap of wild leather that was, in fact, the very skin of its owner. (Little Toniot, to imitate his father, would draw a similar strap upon himself with a ligature, and he would pull the string until it drew blood to ensure that he had cleanly traced out the demarcation.) The man never spoke. He killed animals, was the *mole catcher* of his town. He would set out fox traps, weasel traps, rat traps, poisons, special traps for game, and, because he did not have a hunting license, he would take various precautions, like hanging moles prominently from his jacket, so that they were visible; they were also often rotten and had been so for several weeks.

He had inherited his house, washed up in the clearing of the woods like a castaway upon a deserted island; he lived there in simplicity, catching all that he could eat: the woman and the little boy could not ask for more, because the police would not mix themselves in with his affairs. From time to time, he would go to a very distant neighbouring village, to sell a few woven baskets. Setting off with five, he would always return with one carefully filled with horse manure, so that he might fertilize the vegetables in the garden a bit. He would also buy bread and lard and place them in the middle of the manure, covering it all with an old newspaper, to keep away the flies. He would walk barefoot in the winter and in the summer, for his soles had become as hard as iron. No one knew if he loved his wife. His wife hated him with all of her guts. First, he never spoke, and women have a superstitious fear of silent men; next, he had given her a son, and she would have preferred a daughter, that is to say an ally, an accomplice, a nimbler creature, capable of appreciating all the vain phrases that would escape from exasperated mouths on rainy days. Also, the wife of big

Toniot complained about him, with an abundant torrent of froth, to the rare women whom Providence dared to send her way on Sundays. When the women who collected dead wood, the shepherdesses, the women who collected lilies of the valley, or the peddlers happened to stray all the way to her house, they were subjected to a stream of speeches and lamentations that swept them away, arms waving, from one end of the home to another, the house having found itself instantaneously purged of its two men. Thank God, the big and the small Toniots could flee, the woods were vast; and, when that happened, the ginger woman, weary of the life of laziness that she led amongst her two mean boys ("So mean, Madame, that they snap their beaks, without every saying anything!"), would air her woes and then unsurprisingly find herself unable to sleep serenely next to him because he *stank like a mole* too strongly.

Then, she, because she liked to spend money needlessly, would buy a bundle of mushrooms picked the night prior, a bouquet of lilies of the valley, or one or two spools of thread.

Big Toniot never held this against her, but little Toniot would shake his head, disdainfully. Couldn't they simply collect their own dead wood, their own mushrooms, their own flowers themselves? As for the string, little Toniot knew how to make that, with twigs whose resistance he had already tested many times as he made traps for the birds.

One Sunday, it was a peddler, instead of the wandering seamstress, who sold some string to the wife of big Toniot. That day they spoke less loudly in the empty house... the peddler unfolded his fabrics. It was very interesting. You would have thought you were hearing a bee make his honey, and big Toniot, next week, noticed that someone was stealing his onions.

—How dare you, cried the female as her hair stood on end, how dare you accuse an honest peddler in good standing with the police—he even showed me his sales permit! He doesn't need your onions, you filthy owl! He is a good clean man, who wears leather shoes every day and drinks wine on Sundays.

What she would not admit is that she had offered the onions in exchange for several other shady gestures.

Big Toniot lowered his head, sniffing around the door. Indeed, the scent of wine was present in his house, and he didn't add anything, each word would have been too great a cerebral effort. For the rest, when he was staring at an animal behind a hedge, he didn't have the puerility to subject it to a speech!

But little Toniot naively promised himself to keep an eye on their onions.

That is why, when he heard a cracking near the garden that night, he rose from his bed, as his father slept beneath the hanging rifle, his father, the stinking male relegated by a woman who had become extremely delicate since she decided that she needed a dress and could no longer tolerate the irritating touch of a shirt upon her burning skin...

Alas! Little Toniot now has a fever, he cannot sleep. His time has come to hunt the great beast. He tracks, he listens in the dark. He turns over and over softly upon the dry heather for fear of making too much noise. Every night he waits for something. Something or someone. He does not know exactly which. The index finger of silence burrows deep within his brain. He calculated that every eight days the earth can be heard groaning. The deaf shuddering of a chest upon which a knee is placed, the deep quiverings of revolt which go out with a discreet signal, like the cough of a very old, wise person; and the heart of the earth beats in the chest of the little beast on the lookout, who rises at last, looks straight before him, his nostrils sniffing the trail.

With a lithe movement like a garden snake, little Toniot has reached the door without examining his mother's bed.

He fully understands that Mrs Moon has left. What remains is the canvas shirt left wilting upon the brown blanket, the shroud of the woman who died putting him forth into the world a second time beneath the blows of her powerful fists.

Ah! she made him a man that awful night, and he had felt himself become her enemy forever.

To the hunt!

And he slides outside into the soft blue brightness that bathes him, caresses him, inundates him with courage. The moon is hidden near the pond where the frogs are singing. Yes, the moon is over there upon the first branches of the woods. It is a pretty white shape, round all over, that rolls along atop the grass; it is veiled in a thick cloud that holds it by its belt, looking to eat its head. And it rolls, and it slides, and all the lights escape from there, reflections of red hair, of milky throats. Little Toniot crawls and bends the grass with caution. He has left the garden, he is nearly at the ditch, before the woods where there is something resembling an alcove, a thick layer of greenery. He watches, he watches and laughs silently, despite the discomfort he feels as his heart constricts in a horrible way. What he sees, he will never forget, because it is too funny! He sees a great white frog, yes, it's definitely that, those marvellously flexible thighs and open arms, the precise, springy stretchiness of those members that are so pale that they seem to be made of silver! Now he understands why they call him a toad, it's because he is actually the son of a frog. He watches, he watches, he feels a pain in his eyes as they sting! He will watch this his whole life, within himself, in the deepest part of his heart, he will watch himself as if staring into a poisoned spring whose reflections are both cruel and sweet.

He has finally seen enough! He turns back on his path, that little beast, he retreats, returns to his den. He will perhaps return to bed like a docile, knowing child, his head turned towards the wall, but it is beyond his control, the spirit of the earth, the ancient pact forged between men to protect one another from the Enemy pushes him past his own bed to his father's.

Big Toniot now awakens, sniffing the wind:

— What is it, boy, are you sick?

— No, it's mother, we have to go. Get up now, papa.

He said papa like when he was a newborn, still incapable of a misdeed.

And the father rises, snorts, grumbles:

— What this time? What's wrong with that whore?

— Someone is stealing our onions, I'm sure of it! Little Toniot, his voice as low as his brow, full of disgust before the inexplicable crime that he tries his best to explain.

— Good god!

And the father unhooks the rifle.

— It's the string seller, is it?

— I don't know! There's a man.

— Well I know who it is. Stay here.

The little boy stays. It's not his business. The father knows his job.

And little Toniot goes to lie back down, plugging his ears as he does so. All the same he hears two shots, still within himself, within the depths of his being where forevermore there has been painted the image of the great white frog, of Mrs Moon wallowing upon the ground beneath an unknown cloud. He hears a cry, two cries... and he unplugs his ears. His teeth chatter. By God, what just happened? Is she going to come back, furious, to kill him with her fists?

Indeed, she comes back, dragged by big Toniot who holds her by her hair.

– Boy!, says the father in a gruff voice where one can hear the whole world shuddering in pain, I've brought you back some meat!

The great white frog is streaked across its thighs with splashes of blood that come spilling from its mouth. Its arms and legs flail in nervous movements that imitate those of earlier, for the pains of agony greatly resemble the joys of voluptuousness.

Then she clenches her jaw.

The great white frog will never sing again.

He stayed there alone, feeling rather proud of himself. He spent his days staring at the animals. The policemen, in taking his father from him, left him his rifle. His mother is buried far away. The women who descended upon him, great buzzing horseflies, to offer him eggs, milk, consolations, to take part in the misery of an orphan, all fled because he spoke too frankly about what he thought of chatty people. He cleans his little corner, shakes out his sheet, boils his soup. He has space, they sold nearly everything according to the court, and when the village priest comes, a look of holy smugness on his face, Toniot locks his door and flees through the hole near the chimney. Ah! no, he is the master of his house, and he is no longer a boy from catechism!

Having the good fortune not to owe anything to anyone on earth, it seems needless to him to tolerate threats from heaven. (Also, as soon as it rains, he goes to bed, because it saves him at least one meal!)

Nevertheless, the seasons change. He will have to go and get his fathers' rags, in prison, because his pants are from when he was a boy, and do not want to grow with him. And first he makes two cane baskets, remembering the material that they used to spread out before heading into the city... and the two rabbits they used to hide. The rabbits and the baskets, one within the other, will probably fetch one hundred sous. A fortune. Enough lard for six months.

And so he sets out, heading down various paths at random. No matter what, he will arrive at his destination and he has lots of time. He is on his way, indeed; it's market day in the city. He is talking about big Toniot, the one who killed his wife... Strange thing, everyone knows from what he is returning. That surprises him. There must be many big Toniots who kill their wives, right? He learns that it is less common in the cities than one might think. Woman! There are many more... frogs than men, anyone can guess that, and you would need too much lead.

He finds the prison and obtains his inheritance: the famous pair of cloth pants, now greener than ever, decorated with reddish stars, and the old, short jacket, all patched up. A tender soul takes pity upon him: his father, in short, was perhaps not so guilty; he had acted almost in accordance to his right, and they surely would not have condemned him to forced labour for life if he had been a gentleman of the city, instead of being a savage woodsman and a permit-less hunter. — So, killing a woman, crippling a peddler, these things are not as serious as not possessing a hunting license... This last echo of civilized existence fills him with a new stupor. Everything becomes jumbled in his poor little simpleton mind. He throws his rabbits onto a pile of manure, not daring to sell them. It makes him dizzy. He imagines that he has really thrown aside his father and his mother. He gives his baskets to a passer-by, flees the city as if he had the entire police force on his heels, and he does not breathe again until he is deep within the woods once more. He will still have to live without a hunting license, right? And so, what? He'll have to return to justify the shots he has taken with his personal rifle? He finds a way. Instead of killing rabbits or people, he will fish, and nothing more. The important thing is to remain free. And he laughs silently, thinking of what he will catch...

...For the birds were still singing! As soon as night fell, you could hear them jabbering, gossiping, from the depths of the forest ponds, the little ponds surrounding his house, the beautiful ponds, dingy crystal coupes overflowing with mousse, filled with a mysterious liqueur that is an equal blend of the rotten autumn leaves and the purest honey from the springtime flowers, blue irises, water lilies, pink saggitaria, and periwinkles, dark periwinkles that weave together in braids to ensnare the legs of the animal hunters.

Yes, yes, they were murmuring, the birds, imploring, crying out in the eternal agony of seeking a king, and, as they came together to form disgusting circles, gleaming with the pleasure of being so stupid up there, they were bothering him with their sinister vociferations. From all corners of the woods, on summer evenings, a concert of maledictions would rise, cascading back down in long sobs upon the forehead of the orphan.

Ah! yes, how well he knew then that he would fish! Because one must kill in order to live, it is better to kill soundlessly and that the death that one delivers serves to stifle out all sounds. What intense joy he felt in plucking these living flowers from the dark ponds, which had bloomed in the mouths of mad women... which he would shut one by one.

Returning from the city, little Toniot felt himself to be a big Toniot, a little bit more ferocious than the other, having inherited an abandoned house and a murderer's trousers. And he straightened his back, overcome by a respect for himself, a man who had now found his path. The cane baskets hardly fetch any money, the mushrooms do not last, and the birds are strangely distrustful. The field rat makes for a poor roast, emitting, when cooked, a fetid odour of musk... Whereas a frog... tastes like chicken! An absolute delight! He could see, in his daydreams, the little white thighs all aligned upon a hazelnut skewer, roasting over the fire, and turning slowly with the docility of little, vaguely spectral, puppets. He would eat a lot and sell the rest. No, he would depopulate the countryside of those obnoxious creatures, whose songs, half-prayers, half-oaths, litanies of the hysterical, obsessed his memory horribly.

...Each day Toniot leaves his house where the structure has been ravaged by the winter wind, which carried away the door and a part of the roof. It is no longer his ancestral home, it is his ruin. He lives inside as a night owl takes shelter within the hole of an old wall or rock after a storm. He has lost his taste for light and bread. He shakes himself from his sleep only at the first call from the frogs. Then, he stretches on all fours, wild upon the warpath, his nose raised in the wind. He crawls, he sniffs, he tracks the scents of the forest that the tenderness of the forest wets with his tears. If it is autumn, it smells of rosemary, juniper, and the acorn from the oak tree that emits little bursts of bitterness as it dries. If it is springtime, it smells of sage, elderflower, and the dog rose bush in full bloom.

Either the animals are starting to flee, or they are becoming hopelessly blended.

The only change taking place within the man is that there is a bit more sadness or a bit more languidness.

Nothing can be explained and everything would be a source of such shame, if one were to dwell upon it.

But Toniot is no longer thinking of it. He is far from the cities, far from his parents, far from himself. The pernicious ponds, mirrors that have reflected all the mysteries, call to him, fascinate him, bewitch him. He is the prince of the frogs that hail him, with a frenetic passion... without ever having glimpsed him better than at the moment of their death.

And he will go to them, upon his shoulder a pole where there hangs a thread (perhaps the same once sold to his mother by the peddler!) and a little piece of red cloth the length of a woman's tongue. He goes beneath the boughs, his step methodical, his eye cold and firm, his black hair streaking across his forehead with harsh lines. He looks like a very old man who would possess the same piercing eyes as those of a young animal. Before the shallow pool, he salutes them with a silent laugh. He does not make a speech nor any tidings of good comings. Each, in a great show of their numerical strength, begins undulating in wide bands, and they ripple the surface of the water as if it were a piece of soft silk.

Around them, the trees bow their heads as they contemplate the drama. Their weeping hair unfurls, and the moon, which comes out early when the sky is pure, appears as an amber diadem, growing incrementally darker until it is the colour of blood. Later, it will be like the point of an arrow which will sharpen itself upon the agony of the day.

The clamour of the frogs swells horribly, their yellow eyes, drops of wept gold, glow like stars. From the middle of their sabbath they emit human words, they have sharp interjections such as children who might be amused by the excess would have, or croak themselves hoarse in a puerile rage. They are the little monstrosities born of unmentionable liaisons, tiny foetuses plunged into the universal jar who try to break its clear walls with their desperate little hands.

And now they pile on top of one another, the poor little monsters, to contemplate the red tongue that the man is dangling from the end of his accursed string; the fiery tongue of the chimera! They have fascinated, charming little sirens, and now it is his turn, he fascinates them. The pole rises. The string whips through space, and in the air echoes the atrocious cry of a bird deplumed while still alive. The frog, too curious, is seized by the double hook which, from afar, looks like the anchor of salvation. Its back legs shake like those of a young girl being raped...

Calmly, the frog hunter plucks them one by one.

He seems to be reaping them with the end of his pole. He would take them all if it were possible to take all the frogs from a pond where each drop of scum hides one waiting to be born, and each drop of pure water conceals an adult. But night is coming.

The moon watches, a queen who is mostly indifferent as to what happens to her subjects. Whether the frogs sing or fall silent, it does not stop her from being the only frog eye to have seen everything since the start of the world.

Toniot fills his bag. A long cloth sack that he cut from his mother's last shirt. His nails are red with blood. His fishing concluded, he returns home, his pole upon his shoulder, the sack hanging from it, its belly swollen with small bellies still sighing and exhaling. At home, it's mealtime and he peacefully lights his hearth. The wind whistles, blowing upon the fire. The earth shudders, grumbling gently. No, no one else can stop him from eating his fill, from living. He is free.

On his knees before the pile of small corpses, he strips them, removes the double hook from their golden eyes, removes their lovely dresses of green satin, their cute knickers of white velvet. It all slides here and there like a doll's clothing, and all that remains are their bare thighs, so pale, trembling with nervous shivers...

...And the resolute pupils of the man show a strange flame, a gleam of greed or hate, while in the distance, dogs howl at the moon, dreaming of biting Death on the arse.

INSECTS &
ARACHNIDS

The Caterpillar

JULES RENARD

She emerges from a tuft of grass which had kept her hidden from the day's heat. She crosses the sandy path with grand undulations. She does not stop there and, for a moment, thinks herself lost within the impression left by the gardener's boot.

Arriving at the strawberries, she rests, lifts her nose to the right and to the left, breathing deeply, seeking the trail; then she sets off again, over the leaves and under the leaves, she now knows where she is going.

Such a beautiful caterpillar, plump, velvety, furry, brown with specks of gold and her eyes of black!

She jiggles and furrows like a bushy eyebrow, guided by scent.

She stops at the foot of a rosebush.

With her slender hooks, she tests the rough bark, her head wobbles like a new-born pup, and she resolves to climb.

And, this time, you would say that she swallows, painfully, the path before her as she ascends by lengths.

At the very top of the rosebush, there blooms a rose the colour of an innocent young girl. The perfumes that it puts forth intoxicate her. It resists no one. Its stem is open to the first caterpillar to make the climb. It welcomes her like a gift.

And, sensing that it will be chilly that night, the rose is quite happy to wrap a boa about its neck.

Caterpillars

E. F. BENSON

I saw a month or two ago in an Italian paper that the Villa Cascana, in which I once stayed, had been pulled down, and that a manufactory of some sort was in process of erection on its site. There is therefore no longer any reason for refraining from writing of those things which I myself saw (or imagined I saw) in a certain room and on a certain landing of the villa in question, nor from mentioning the circumstances which followed, which may or may not (according to the opinion of the reader) throw some light on or be somehow connected with this experience.

The Villa Cascana was in all ways but one a perfectly delightful house, yet, if it were standing now, nothing in the world — I use the phrase in its literal sense — would induce me to set foot in it again, for I believe it to have been haunted in a very terrible and practical manner. Most ghosts, when all is said and done, do not do much harm; they may perhaps terrify, but the person whom they visit usually gets over their visitation. They may on the other hand be entirely friendly and beneficent. But the appearances in the Villa Cascana were not beneficent, and had they made their 'visit' in a very slightly different manner, I do not suppose I should have got over it any more than Arthur Inglis did.

The house stood on an ilex-clad hill not far from Sestri di Levante on the Italian Riviera, looking out over the iridescent blues of that enchanted sea, while behind it rose the pale green chestnut woods that climb up the hillsides 'till they give place to the pines that, black in contrast with them, crown the slopes. All round it the garden in the luxuriance of mid-spring bloomed and was fragrant, and the scent of magnolia and rose, borne on the salt freshness of the winds from the sea, flowed like a stream through the cool vaulted rooms.

On the ground floor a broad pillared loggia ran round three sides of the house, the top of which formed a balcony for certain rooms of the first floor. The main staircase, broad and of grey marble steps, led up from the hall to the landing outside these rooms, which were three in number, namely, two big sitting-rooms and a bedroom arranged en suite. The latter was unoccupied, the sitting-rooms were in use. From these the main staircase was continued to the second floor, where were situated certain bedrooms, one of which I occupied, while from the other side of the first-floor landing some half-dozen steps led to another suite of rooms, where, at the time I am speaking of, Arthur Inglis, the artist, had his bedroom and studio. Thus the landing outside my bedroom at the top of the house commanded both the landing of the first floor and also the steps that led to Inglis' rooms. Jim Stanley and his wife, finally (whose guest I was), occupied rooms in another wing of the house, where also were the servants' quarters.

I arrived just in time for lunch on a brilliant noon of mid-May. The garden was shouting with colour and fragrance, and not less delightful after my broiling walk up from the marina, should have been the coming from the reverberating heat and blaze of the day into the marble coolness of the villa. Only (the reader has my bare word for this, and nothing more), the moment I set foot in the house I felt that something was wrong. This feeling, I may say, was quite vague, though very strong, and I remember that when I saw letters waiting for me on the table in the hall I felt certain that the explanation was here: I was convinced that there was bad news of some sort for me. Yet when I opened them I found no such explanation of my premonition: my correspondents all reeked of prosperity. Yet this clear miscarriage of a presentiment did not dissipate my uneasiness. In that cool fragrant house there was something wrong.

I am at pains to mention this because to the general view it may explain that though I am as a rule so excellent a sleeper that the extinction of my light on getting into bed is apparently contemporaneous with being called on the following morning, I slept very badly on my first night in the Villa Cascana. It may also explain the fact that when I did sleep (if it was indeed in sleep that I saw what I thought I saw) I dreamed in a very vivid and original manner, original, that is to say, in the sense that something that, as far as I knew, had never previously entered into my consciousness, usurped it then. But since, in addition to this evil premonition, certain words and events occurring during the rest of the day might have suggested something of what I thought happened that night, it will be well to relate them.

After lunch, then, I went round the house with Mrs Stanley, and during our tour she referred, it is true, to the unoccupied bedroom on the first floor, which opened out of the room where we had lunched.

"We left that unoccupied," she said, "because Jim and I have a charming bedroom and dressing-room, as you saw, in the wing, and if we used it ourselves we should have to turn the dining-room into a dressing-room and have our meals downstairs. As it is, however, we have our little flat there, Arthur Inglis has his little flat in the other passage; and I remembered (aren't I extraordinary?) that you once said that the higher up you were in a house the better you were pleased. So I put you at the top of the house, instead of giving you that room."

It is true, that a doubt, vague as my uneasy premonition, crossed my mind at this. I did not see why Mrs Stanley should have explained all this, if there had not been more to explain. I allow, therefore, that the thought that there was something to explain about the unoccupied bedroom was momentarily present to my mind.

The second thing that may have borne on my dream was this.

At dinner the conversation turned for a moment on ghosts. Inglis, with the certainty of conviction, expressed his belief that anybody who could possibly believe in the existence of supernatural phenomena was unworthy of the name of an ass. The subject instantly dropped. As far as I can recollect, nothing else occurred or was said that could bear on what follows.

We all went to bed rather early, and personally I yawned my way upstairs, feeling hideously sleepy. My room was rather hot, and I threw all the windows wide, and from without poured in the white light of the moon, and the love-song of many nightingales. I undressed quickly, and got into bed, but though I had felt so sleepy before, I now felt extremely wide-awake. But I was quite content to be awake: I did not toss or turn, I felt perfectly happy listening to the song and seeing the light. Then, it is possible, I may have gone to sleep, and what follows may have been a dream. I thought, anyhow, that after a time the nightingales ceased singing and the moon sank. I thought also that if, for some unexplained reason, I was going to lie awake all night, I might as well read, and I remembered that I had left a book in which I was interested in the dining-room on the first floor. So I got out of bed, lit a candle, and went downstairs. I went into the room, saw on a side-table the book I had come to look for, and then, simultaneously, saw that the door into the unoccupied bedroom was open. A curious grey light, not of dawn nor of moonshine, came out of it, and I looked in. The bed stood just opposite the door, a big four-poster, hung with tapestry at the head. Then I saw that the greyish light of the bedroom came from the bed, or rather from what was on the bed. For it was covered with great caterpillars, a foot or more in length, which crawled over it. They were faintly luminous, and it was the light from them that showed me the room. Instead of the sucker-feet of ordinary caterpillars they had rows of pincers like crabs, and they moved by grasping what they lay on with their pincers, and then sliding their bodies forward. In colour these dreadful insects were yellowish-grey, and they were covered with irregular lumps and swellings. There must have been hundreds of them, for they formed a sort of writhing, crawling pyramid on the bed. Occasionally one fell off on to the floor, with a soft fleshy thud, and though the floor was of hard concrete, it yielded to the pincerfeet as if it had been putty, and, crawling back, the caterpillar would mount on to the bed again, to rejoin its fearful companions. They appeared to have no faces, so to speak, but at one end of them there was a mouth that opened sideways in respiration.

Then, as I looked, it seemed to me as if they all suddenly became conscious of my presence. All the mouths, at any rate, were turned in my direction, and next moment they began dropping off the bed with those soft fleshy thuds on to the floor, and wriggling towards me. For one second a paralysis as of a dream was on me, but the next I was running upstairs again to my room, and I remember feeling the cold of the marble steps on my bare feet. I rushed into my bedroom, and slammed the door behind me, and then — I was certainly wide-awake now — I found myself standing by my bed with the sweat of terror pouring from me. The noise of the banged door still rang in my ears. But, as would have been more usual, if this had been mere nightmare, the terror that had been mine when I saw those foul beasts crawling about the bed or dropping softly on to the floor did not cease then. Awake, now, if dreaming before, I did not at all recover from the horror of dream: it did not seem to me that I had dreamed. And until dawn, I sat or stood, not daring to lie down, thinking that every rustle or movement that I heard was the approach of the caterpillars. To them and the claws that bit into the cement the wood of the door was child's play: steel would not keep them out.

But with the sweet and noble return of day the horror vanished: the whisper of wind became benignant again: the nameless fear, whatever it was, was smoothed out and terrified me no longer. Dawn broke, hueless at first; then it grew dove-coloured, then the flaming pageant of light spread over the sky.

The admirable rule of the house was that everybody had breakfast where and when he pleased, and in consequence it was not 'till lunch-time that I met any of the other members of our party, since I had breakfast on my balcony, and wrote letters and other things till lunch. In fact, I got down to that meal rather late, after the other three had begun. Between my knife and fork there was a small pill-box of cardboard, and as I sat down Inglis spoke.

"Do look at that," he said, "since you are interested in natural history. I found it crawling on my counterpane last night, and I don't know what it is."

I think that before I opened the pill-box I expected something of the sort which I found in it. Inside it, anyhow, was a small caterpillar, greyish-yellow in colour, with curious bumps and excrescences on its rings. It was extremely active, and hurried round the box, this way and that. Its feet were unlike the feet of any caterpillar I ever saw: they were like the pincers of a crab. I looked, and shut the lid down again.

"No, I don't know it," I said, "but it looks rather unwholesome. What are you going to do with it?"

"Oh, I shall keep it," said Inglis. "It has begun to spin: I want to see what sort of a moth it turns into."

I opened the box again, and saw that these hurrying movements were indeed the beginning of the spinning of the web of its cocoon. Then Inglis spoke again.

"It has got funny feet, too," he said. "They are like crabs' pincers. What's the Latin for crab? Oh, yes, Cancer. So in case it is unique, let's christen it: 'Cancer Inglisensis'."

Then something happened in my brain, some momentary piecing together of all that I had seen or dreamed. Something in his words seemed to me to throw light on it all, and my own intense horror at the experience of the night before linked itself on to what he had just said. In effect, I took the box and threw it, caterpillar and all, out of the window. There was a gravel path just outside, and beyond it, a fountain playing into a basin. The box fell on to the middle of this.

Inglis laughed.

"So the students of the occult don't like solid facts," he said. "My poor caterpillar!"

The talk went off again at once on to other subjects, and I have only given in detail, as they happened, these trivialities in order to be sure myself that I have recorded everything that could have borne on occult subjects or on the subject of caterpillars. But at the moment when I threw the pill-box into the fountain, I lost my head: my only excuse is that, as is probably plain, the tenant of it was, in miniature, exactly what I had seen crowded on to the bed in the unoccupied room. And though this translation of those phantoms into flesh and blood — or whatever it is that caterpillars are made of — ought perhaps to have relieved the horror of the night, as a matter of fact it did nothing of the kind. It only made the crawling pyramid that covered the bed in the unoccupied room more hideously real.

After lunch we spent a lazy hour or two strolling about the garden or sitting in the loggia, and it must have been about four o'clock when Stanley and I started off to bathe, down the path that led by the fountain into which I had thrown the pill-box. The water was shallow and clear, and at the bottom of it I saw its white remains. The water had disintegrated the cardboard, and it had become no more than a few strips and shreds of sodden paper. The centre of the fountain was a marble Italian Cupid which squirted the water out of a wine-skin held under its arm. And crawling up its leg was the caterpillar. Strange and scarcely credible as it seemed, it must have survived the falling-to-bits of its prison, and made it's way to shore, and there it was, out of arm's reach, weaving and waving this way and that as it evolved its cocoon.

Then, as I looked at it, it seemed to me again that, like the caterpillar I had seen last night, it saw me, and breaking out of the threads that surrounded it, it crawled down the marble leg of the Cupid and began swimming like a snake across the water of the fountain towards me. It came with extraordinary speed (the fact of a caterpillar being able to swim was new to me), and in another moment was crawling up the marble lip of the basin. Just then Inglis joined us.

"Why, if it isn't old 'Cancer Inglisensis' again," he said, catching sight of the beast. "What a tearing hurry it is in!"

We were standing side by side on the path, and when the caterpillar had advanced to within about a yard of us, it stopped, and began waving again as if in doubt as to the direction in which it should go. Then it appeared to make up its mind, and crawled on to Inglis' shoe.

"It likes me best," he said, "but I don't really know that I like it. And as it won't drown I think perhaps —"

He shook it off his shoe on to the gravel path and trod on it.

All afternoon the air got heavier and heavier with the Sirocco that was without doubt coming up from the south, and that night again I went up to bed feeling very sleepy; but below my drowsiness, so to speak, there was the consciousness, stronger than before, that there was something wrong in the house, that something dangerous was close at hand. But I fell asleep at once, and — how long after I do not know — either woke or dreamed I awoke, feeling that I must get up at once, or *I should be too late*. Then (dreaming or awake) I lay and fought this fear, telling myself that I was but the prey of my own nerves disordered by Sirocco or what not, and at the same time quite clearly knowing in another part of my mind, so to speak, that every moment's delay added to the danger. At last this second feeling became irresistible, and I put on coat and trousers and went out of my room on to the landing. And then I saw that I had already delayed too long, and that I was now too late.

The whole of the landing of the first floor below was invisible under the swarm of caterpillars that crawled there. The folding doors into the sitting-room from which opened the bedroom where I had seen them last night were shut, but they were squeezing through the cracks of it and dropping one by one through the keyhole, elongating themselves into mere string as they passed, and growing fat and lumpy again on emerging. Some, as if exploring, were nosing about the steps into the passage at the end of which were Inglis' rooms, others were crawling on the lowest steps of the staircase that led up to where I stood. The landing, however, was completely covered with them: I was cut off. And of the frozen horror that seized me when I saw that I can give no idea in words.

Then at last a general movement began to take place, and they grew thicker on the steps that led to Inglis' room. Gradually, like some hideous tide of flesh, they advanced along the passage, and I saw the foremost, visible by the pale grey luminousness that came from them, reach his door. Again and again I tried to shout and warn him, in terror all the time that they would turn at the sound of my voice and mount my stair instead, but for all my efforts I felt that no sound came from my throat. They crawled along the hinge-crack of his door, passing through as they had done before, and still I stood there, making impotent efforts to shout to him, to bid him escape while there was time.

At last the passage was completely empty: they had all gone, and at that moment I was conscious for the first time of the cold of the marble landing on which I stood barefooted. The dawn was just beginning to break in the Eastern sky.

Six months after I met Mrs Stanley in a country house in England. We talked on many subjects and at last she said:

"I don't think I have seen you since I got that dreadful news about Arthur Inglis a month ago."

"I haven't heard," said I.

"No? He has got cancer. They don't even advise an operation, for there is no hope of a cure: he is riddled with it, the doctors say."

Now during all these six months I do not think a day had passed on which I had not had in my mind the dreams (or whatever you like to call them) which I had seen in the Villa Cascana.

"It is awful, is it not?" she continued, "and I feel I can't help feeling, that he may have —"

"Caught it at the villa?" I asked.

She looked at me in blank surprise.

"Why did you say that?" she asked. "How did you know?"

Then she told me. In the unoccupied bedroom a year before there had been a fatal case of cancer. She had, of course, taken the best advice and had been told that the utmost dictates of prudence would be obeyed so long as she did not put anybody to sleep in the room, which had also been thoroughly disinfected and newly white-washed and painted. But —

To a Moth That Drinketh of the Ripe October

EMILY PFEIFFER

I.

A moth belated, — sun and zephyr-kist, —
Trembling about a pale arbutus bell,
Probing to wildering depths its honeyed cell, —
A noonday thief, a downy sensualist!
Not vainly, sprite, thou drawest careless breath,
Strikest ambrosia from the cool-cupped flowers,
And flutterest through the soft, uncounted hours,
To drop at last in unawaited death; —
'Tis something to be glad! and those fine thrills
Which move thee, to my lip have drawn the smile
Wherewith we look on joy. Drink! drown thine ills,
If ill have any part in thee; erewhile
May the pent force — thy bounded life — set free,
Fill larger sphere with equal ecstasy!

II.

With what fine organs art thou dowered, frail elf!
Thy harp is pitched too high for dull annoy,
Thy life a love-feast, and a silent joy,
As mute and rapt as Passion's silent self.
I turn from thee, and see the swallow sweep
Like a winged will, and the keen-scented hound
That snuffs with rapture at the tainted ground, —
All things that freely course, that swim or leap, —
Then, hearing glad-voiced creatures men call dumb,
I feel my heart — oft sinking 'neath the weight
Of Nature's sorrow — lighten at the sum
Of Nature's joy; its half-unfolded fate
Breathes hope — for all but those beneath the ban
Of the inquisitor and tyrant, man.

A Dream of Wild Bees

(written as a letter to a friend)

OLIVE SCHREINER

A mother sat alone at an open window. Through
it came the voices of the children as they played
under the acacia-trees, and the breath of the
hot afternoon air. In and out of the room flew the bees, the
wild bees, with their legs yellow with pollen, going to and
from the acacia-trees, droning all the while. She sat on a
low chair before the table and darned. She took her work
from the great basket that stood before her on the table:
some lay on her knee and half covered the book that rested
there. She watched the needle go in and out; and the dreary
hum of the bees and the noise of the children's voices

became a confused murmur in her ears, as she worked slowly and more slowly. Then the bees, the long-legged wasp-like fellows who make no honey, flew closer and closer to her head, droning. Then she grew more and more drowsy, and she laid her hand, with the stocking over it, on the edge of the table, and leaned her head upon it. And the voices of the children outside grew more and more dreamy, came now far, now near; then she did not hear them, but she felt under her heart where the ninth child lay. Bent forward and sleeping there, with the bees flying about her head, she had a weird brain-picture; she thought the bees lengthened and lengthened themselves out and became human creatures and moved round and round her. Then one came to her softly, saying, "Let me lay my hand upon thy side where the child sleeps. If I shall touch him he shall be as I."

She asked, "Who are you?"

And he said, "I am Health. Whom I touch will have always the red blood dancing in his veins; he will not know weariness nor pain; life will be a long laugh to him."

"No," said another, "let me touch; for I am Wealth. If I touch him material care shall not feed on him. He shall live on the blood and sinews of his fellow-men, if he will; and what his eye lusts for, his hand will have. He shall not know 'I want.'" And the child lay still like lead.

And another said, "Let me touch him: I am Fame. The man I touch, I lead to a high hill where all men may see him. When he dies he is not forgotten, his name rings down the centuries, each echoes it on to his fellows. Think — not to be forgotten through the ages!"

And the mother lay breathing steadily, but in the brain-picture they pressed closer to her.

"Let me touch the child," said one, "for I am Love. If I touch him he shall not walk through life alone. In the greatest dark, when he puts out his hand he shall find another hand by it. When the world is against him, another shall say, 'You and I.'" And the child trembled.

But another pressed close and said, "Let me touch; for I am Talent. I can do all things — that have been done before. I touch the soldier, the statesman, the thinker, and the politician who succeed; and the writer who is never before his time, and never behind it. If I touch the child he shall not weep for failure."

About the mother's head the bees were flying, touching her with their long tapering limbs; and, in her brain-picture, out of the shadow of the room came one with sallow face, deep-lined, the cheeks drawn into hollows, and a mouth smiling quiveringly. He stretched out his hand. And the mother drew back, and cried, "Who are you?" He answered nothing; and she looked up between his eyelids. And she said, "What can you give the child — health?" And he said, "The man I touch, there wakes up in his blood a burning fever, that shall lick his blood as fire. The fever that I will give him shall be cured when his life is cured."

"You give wealth?"

He shook his head. "The man whom I touch, when he bends to pick up gold, he sees suddenly a light over his head in the sky; while he looks up to see it, the gold slips from between his fingers, or sometimes another passing takes it from them."

"Fame?"

He answered, "likely not. For the man I touch there is a path traced out in the sand by a finger which no man sees. That he must follow. Sometimes it leads almost to the top, and then turns down suddenly into the valley. He must follow it, though none else sees the tracing."

"Love?"

He said, "He shall hunger for it — but he shall not find it. When he stretches out his arms to it, and would lay his heart against a thing he loves, then, far off along the horizon he shall see a light play. He must go towards it. The thing he loves will not journey with him; he must travel alone. When he presses somewhat to his burning heart, crying, 'Mine, mine, my own!' he shall hear a voice — 'Renounce! renounce! this is not thine!'"

"He shall succeed?"

He said, "He shall fail. When he runs with others they shall reach the goal before him. For strange voices shall call to him and strange lights shall beckon him, and he must wait and listen. And this shall be the strangest: far off across the burning sands where, to other men, there is only the desert's waste, he shall see a blue sea! On that sea the sun shines always, and the water is blue as burning amethyst, and the foam is white on the shore. A great land rises from it, and he shall see upon the mountain-tops burning gold."

The mother said, "He shall reach it?"

And he smiled curiously.

She said, "It is real?"

And he said, "What is real?"

And she looked up between his half-closed eyelids, and said, "Touch."

And he leaned forward and laid his hand upon the sleeper, and whispered to it, smiling; and this only she heard — *"This shall be thy reward — that the ideal shall be real to thee."*

And the child trembled; but the mother slept on heavily and her brain-picture vanished. But deep within her the antenatal thing that lay here had a dream. In those eyes that had never seen the day, in that half-shaped brain was a sensation of light! Light — that it never had seen. Light — that perhaps it never should see. Light — that existed somewhere!

And already it had its reward: the Ideal was real to it.

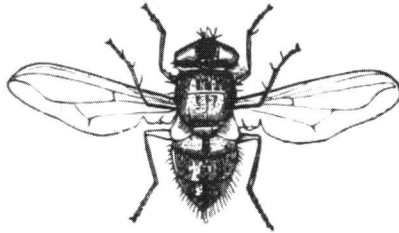

The Golden Fly

ALGERNON BLACKWOOD

t fell upon him out of a clear sky just when existence seemed on its very best behaviour, and he savagely resented the undeserved affliction of it. Involving him in an atrocious scandal that reflected directly upon his honour, it destroyed in a moment the erection his entire life had so laboriously built up — his reputation. In the eyes of the world he was a broken, discredited man, at the very moment, moreover, when his most cherished ambitions touched fulfilment. And the cruelty of it appalled his sense of justice, for it was impossible to vindicate himself without inculpating others who were dearer to him than life. It seemed more than he could bear; and the grim course he contemplated — decision itself as yet hung darkly waiting in the background — appeared the only way of escape that offered.

He had discussed the matter with friends until his brain whirled. Their sympathy maddened him, with hints of *qui s'excuse s'accuse*, and he turned at last in desperation to something that could not answer back. For the first time in his life he turned to Nature — to that dead, inanimate Nature he had left to poets and rhapsodising women: 'I must face it alone,' he put it. For the Finger of God was a phrase without meaning to him, and his entire being contained no trace of the religious instinct. He was a businessman, honest, selfish, and ambitious; and the collapse of his worldly position was paramount to the collapse of the universe itself — his universe, at any rate. This 'crumbling of the universe' was the thought he took out with him. He left the house by the path that led into solitude, and reached the heathery expanse that formed one of the breathing-places of the New Forest. There he flung himself down wearily in the shadow of a little pine-copse. And his crumbled universe lay down with him, for he could not escape it.

Taking the pistol from the hip-pocket where it hurt him, he lay upon his back and watched the clouds. Half stunned, half dazed, he stared into the sky. The perfumed wind played softly on his eyes; he smelt the heather-honey; golden flies hung motionless in the air, like coloured pins fastening the sunshine against the blue curtain of the summer, while dragonflies, like darting shuttles, wove across its pattern their threads of gleaming bronze. He heard the petulant crying of the peewits, and watched their tumbling flight. Below him tinkled a rivulet, its brown water rippling between banks of peaty earth. Everywhere was singing, peace, and careless unconcern.

And this lordly indifference of Nature calmed and soothed him. Neither human pain nor the injustice of man could shift the key of the water, alter the peewits' cry a single tone, nor influence one fraction of an inch those cloudy frigates of vapour that sailed the sky. The earth bulged sunwards as she had bulged for centuries. The power of her steady gait, superbly calm, breathed everywhere with grandeur — undismayed, unhasting, and supremely confident... And, like the flash of those golden flies, there leaped suddenly upon him this vivid thought: that his world of agony lay neatly buttoned up within the tiny space of his own brain. Outside himself it had no existence at all. His mind contained it — the minute interior he called his heart. From this vaster world about him it lay utterly apart, like deeds in the black boxes of japanned tin he kept at the office, shut off from the universe, huddled in an overcrowded space within his skull.

How this commonplace thought reached him, garbed in such startling novelty, was odd enough; for it seemed as though the fierceness of his pain had burned away something. His thoughts it merely enflamed; but this other thing it consumed. Something that had obscured clear vision shrivelled before it as a piece of paper, eaten up by fire, dwindles down into a thimbleful of unimportant ashes. The thicket of his mind grew half transparent. At the farther end he saw, for the first time — light. The perspective of his inner life, hitherto so enormous, telescoped into the proportions of a miniature. Just as momentous and significant as before, it was somehow abruptly different — seen from another point of view. The suffering had burned up rubbish he himself had piled over the head of a little Fact. Like a point of metal that glows yet will not burn, he discerned in the depths of him the essential shining fact that not all this ruinous conflagration could destroy. And this brilliant, indestructible kernel was — his Innocence. The rest was self-reared rubbish: opinion of the world. He had magnified an atom into a universe...

Pain, as it seemed, had cleared a way for the sublimity of Nature to approach him. The calm old Universe rolled past. The deep, majestic Day gave him a push, as though the shoulder of some star had brushed his own. He had thought his feelings were the world: instead, they were merely his way of looking at it. The actual 'world' was some glorious, unchanging thing he never saw direct. His attitude of mind was but a peephole into it. The choice of his particular peephole, moreover, lay surely within the power of his individual will. The anguish, centred upon so small a point, had seemed to affect the entire spread universe around him, whereas in reality it affected nothing but his attitude of mind towards it. The truism struck him like a blow between the eyes, that a man is what he thinks or feels himself to be. It leaped the barrier between words and meaning. The intellectual concept became a hard-edged fact, because he realised it — for the first time in his very circumscribed life. And this dreadful pain that had made even suicide seem desirable was entirely a fabrication of his own mind. The universe about him rolled on just the same in the majesty of its eternal purpose. His tiny inner world was clouded, but the glory of this stupendous world about him was undimmed, untroubled, unaffected. Even death itself...

With a swift smash of the hand he crushed the golden fly that settled on his knee. The murder was done impulsively, utterly without intention. He watched the little point of gold quiver for a moment among the hairs of the rough tweed; then lie still for ever... but the scent of heather-honey filled the air as before; the wind passed sighing through the pines; the clouds still sailed their uncharted sea of blue. There lay the whole spread surface of the Forest in the sun. Only the attitude of the golden fly towards it all was gone. A single, tiny point of view had disappeared. Nature passed on calmly and unhasting; she took no note.

Then, with a rush of awe, another thought flashed through him: Nature had taken note. There was a difference everywhere. Not a sparrow falleth, he remembered, without God knowing. God was certainly in Nature somewhere. His clumsy senses could not register this difference, yet it was there. His own small world, fed by these senses, was after all the merest little corner of Existence. To the whole of Existence, that included himself, the golden fly, the sun, and all the stars, he must somehow answer for his crime. It was a wanton interference with a sublime and sovereign Purpose that he now divined for the first time. He looked at the wee point of gold lying still and silent in the forest of hairs. He realised the enormity of his act. It could not have been graver had he put out the sun, or the little, insignificant flame of his own existence. He had done a criminal, evil thing, for he had put an end to a certain point of view; had wiped it out; made it impossible. Had the fly been quicker, less easily overwhelmed, or more tenacious of the scrap of universal life it used, Nature would at this instant be richer for its little contribution to the whole of things — to which he himself also belonged. And wherein, he asked himself, did he differ from that fly in the importance, the significance of his contribution to the universe? The soul...? He had never given the question a single thought; but if the scrap of life he owned was called a soul, why should that point of golden glory not comprise one too? Its minute size, its trivial purpose, its few hours of apparently futile existence... these formed no true criterion...!

Similarly, the thought rushed over him, a Hand was being stretched out to crush himself. His pain was the shadow of its approach; anger in his heart, the warning. Unless he were quick enough, adroit and skilled enough, he also would be wiped out, while Nature continued her slow, unhasting way without him. His attitude towards the personal pain was really the test of his ability, of his merit — of his right to survive. Pain teaches, pain develops, pain brings growth: he had heard it since his copybook days. But now he realised it, as again thought leaped the barrier between familiar words and meaning. In his attitude of mind to his catastrophe lay his salvation or his... death.

In some such confused and blundering fashion, because along unaccustomed channels, the truth charged into him to overwhelm, yet bringing with it an unwonted sense of joy that seemed to break a crust which long had held back — life. Thus tapped, these sources gushed forth and bubbled over, spread about his being, flooded him with hope and courage, above all with — calmness. Nature held forces just as real and living as human sympathy, and equally able to modify the soul. And Nature was always accessible. A sense of huge companionship, denied him by the littleness of his fellow-men, stole sweetly over him. It was amazingly uplifting, yet fear came close behind it, as he realised the presumption of his former attitude of cynical indifference. These Powers were aware of his petty insolence, yet had not crushed him... It was, of course, the awakening of the religious instinct in a man who hitherto had worshipped merely a rather low-grade form of intellect.

And, while the enormous confusion of it shook him, this sense of incommunicable sweetness remained. Bright haunting eyes, with love in them, gazed at him from the blue; and this thing that came so close, stood also far away upon the line of the horizon. It was everywhere. It filled the hollows, but towered over him as well towards the pinnaces of cloud. It was in the sharpness of the peewits' cry, and in the water's murmur. It whispered in the pine-boughs, and blazed in every patch of sunlight. And it was glory, pure and simple. It filled him with a sense of strength for which he could find but one description — Triumph.

And so, first, the anger faded from his mind and crept away. Resentment then slunk after it. Revolt and disappointment also melted, and bitterness gave place to the most marvellous peace the man had ever known. Then came resignation to fill the empty places. Pain, as a means and not an end, had cleared the way, though the accomplishment was like a miracle. But Conversion is a miracle. No ordinary pain can bring it. This anguish he understood now in a new relation to life — as something to be taken willingly into himself and dealt with, all regardless of public opinion. What people said and thought was in their world, not in his. It was less than nothing. The pain cultivated dormant tracts. The terror also purged. It disclosed...

He watched the wind, and even the wind brought revelation; for without obstacles in its path it would be silent. He watched the sunshine, and the sunshine taught him too; for without obstacles to fling it back against his eye, he could never see it. He would neither hear the tinkling water nor feel the summer heat unless both one and other overcame some reluctant medium in their pathways. And, similarly with his moral being — his pain resulted from the friction of his personal ambitions against the stress of some noble Power that sought to lift him higher. That Power he could not know direct, but he recognised its strain against him by the resistance it generated in the inertia of his selfishness. His attitude of mind had switched completely round. It was what the preachers termed development through suffering.

Moreover, he had acquired this energy of resistance somehow from the wind and sun and the beauty of a common summer's day. Their peace and strength had passed into himself. Unconsciously on his way home he drew upon it steadily. He tossed the pistol into a pool of water. Nature had healed him; and Nature, should he turn weak again, was always there. It was very wonderful. He wanted to sing...

BREAMORE.

The Study of a Spider

JOHN BYRNE LEICESTER WARREN

From holy flower to holy flower
Thou weavest thine unhallowed bower.
The harmless dewdrops, beaded thin,
Ripple along thy ropes of sin.
Thy house a grave, a gulf thy throne
Affright the fairies every one.
Thy winding sheets are grey and fell,
Imprisoning with nets of hell
The lovely births that winnow by,
Winged sisters of the rainbow sky:
Elf-darlings, fluffy, bee-bright things,
And owl-white moths with mealy wings,
And tiny flies, as gauzy thin

As e'er were shut electrum in.
These are thy death spoils, insect ghoul,
With their dear life thy fangs are foul.
Thou felon anchorite of pain
Who sittest in a world of slain.
Hermit, who tunest song unsweet
To heaving wing and writhing feet.
A glutton of creation's sighs,
Miser of many miseries.
Toper, whose lonely feasting chair
Sways in inhospitable air.
The board is bare, the bloated host
Drinks to himself toast after toast.
His lip requires no goblet brink,
But like a weasel must he drink.
The vintage is as old as time
And bright as sunset, pressed and prime.

Ah, venom mouth and shaggy thighs
And paunch grown sleek with sacrifice,
Thy dolphin back and shoulders round
Coarse-hairy, as some goblin hound
Whom a hag rides to sabbath on,
While shuddering stars in fear grow wan.
Thou palace priest of treachery,
Thou type of selfish lechery,
I break the toils around thy head
And from their gibbets take thy dead.

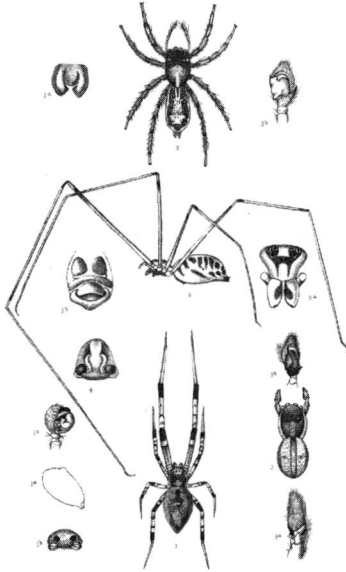

Arachne

MARCEL SCHWOB

Her wagon-spokes made of long spinners' legs;
The cover, of the wings of grasshoppers;
Her traces of the smallest spider's web;
Her collars of the moonshine's watery beams...
Shakespeare, *Romeo and Juliet*

Y ou say that I am mad and you have locked me away; but I care nothing for your precautions and your terrors. For I shall be made free the day that I wish; I shall flee far from your guardians and your gates, dashing along a thread of silk, cast down to me by Arachne. But that hour has not yet come — though it is close: evermore does my heart grow weak and my blood pale. You believe me mad now, you will believe me dead: but I will be dashing along Arachne's string, far beyond the stars.

If I were mad, I would not know what happened so clearly, I would not recall with such precision that which you refer to as my crime, nor the speeches of your lawyers, nor the sentence of your red judge. I would not laugh at the reports of your doctors, and I would not see upon the ceiling of my cell the clean face, the black riding coat, and the white tie of the idiot who decreed me irresponsible. No, I would not see it — for madmen are incapable of forming precise ideas; I, however, pursue my reasonings with clear logic and an extraordinary brightness which surprise even myself. And madmen suffer from pains at the top of their skulls; they believe — poor fools! — that columns of smoke spurt, swirling, from their occiputs. While, in my case, my brain is so light that I feel as if my head were empty. The novels that I have read, which I used to enjoy immensely, I now pass over with a mere glance and I judge them for what they are worth; I see each error of their composition — while the symmetry of my own inventions is so perfect that you would be dazzled if I were to show them to you.

But I despise you infinitely; you could never understand them. I leave you these lines as the final testament of my grievances and so that you will appreciate your own insanity when you find my cell deserted.

Ariana, pale Ariana from whom you took me, was a seamstress. This was the cause of her death. This will be the cause of my salvation. I loved her with intense passion; she was small, brown of skin, and nimble with her fingers; her kisses were pin pricks, her caresses, exhilarating embroideries. And seamstresses have such little lives and are so quick to capriciousness that I was nearing the point of asking her to leave her profession. But she resisted me; and I grew exasperated as I watched the young, tieless, pomaded men who kept a watchful eye over the door of her workshop. My annoyance grew such that I tried to force myself to reprise those old studies which had brought me so much joy.

I endeavoured to read volume XIII of *Asiatic Research*, published in Calcutta in 1820. And automatically fell upon an article about the Phânsigâr. This brought me to the Thuggee.

Captain Sleeman spoke at length about them. Colonel Meadows Taylor was able to glean the secret of their association. They were united amongst themselves by mysterious ties and acted as domestic servants in country estates. In the evening, at dinner, they stupefied their masters with a hemp elixir. At night, climbing along the walls, they slid into open windows by the light of the moon and silently strangled the masters of the house. Their cords were also of hemp, with a great knot at the end so that they might kill more quickly.

Thus, through Hemp, the Thuggee were able to unite sleep and death. The plant that provided hashish which the wealthy used to drug and dull them as with alcohol or opium was also the instrument of their vengeance. The idea then came to me that in punishing my seamstress Ariana with Silk, I would bind her to me completely in death. And this idea, built upon sound logic, became the lodestar of my thoughts. I was unable to resist it for long. When she laid her bent head upon my neck to sleep, I slipped the small cord of silk that I had taken from her basket about her neck; and, tightening it slowly, I drank her last breath from her final kiss.

And this is how you found us, mouth to mouth. You believed me mad and she dead. For you cannot understand that she is with me always, eternally faithful, for she is the nymph Arachne. Day after day, here, in my white cell, she has awakened within me, since that moment when I saw a spider spinning its web above my bed: it was small, its fur brown, and its feet nimble.

The first night, she came down to me, descending a long thread; suspended above my eyes, she embroidered before my pupils a canvas both silken and sombre, with iridescent reflection and luminous purple flowers. Then, next to my body, I felt the nervous, huddled body of Ariana. She kissed me upon my breast, upon the spot that covers the heart — and I cried at the burning sensation. And, for a long time, without so much as a word, we kissed.

The second night, she stretched above me a phosphorescent veil scattered with green stars and yellow circles, strewn shining points that played gaily amongst themselves, growing and shrinking and trembling in the distance. And, kneeling upon my breast, she closed my mouth with her hand; in a long kiss upon my heart, she bit my flesh and sucked my blood until I had been pulled into the void of collapse.

The third night, she covered my eyes with a piece of Marathi silk upon which multi-coloured spiders danced with sparkling eyes. And she squeezed my throat with an endless thread; and violently pulled my heart to her lips through the gaping wound of her bite. Then she slid into my arms and advanced towards my ear to murmur unto me: "I am the nymph Arachne!"

Assuredly, I am not mad; for I immediately understood that my seamstress Ariana was a mortal goddess, and that for the whole of eternity, I had been destined to lead her beyond the labyrinth of humanity with her thread of silk. And the nymph Arachne is grateful to me for having delivered her from her human chrysalis. With boundless precaution, she has swaddled my heart, my poor heart, in her sticky thread; she has wrapped it round a thousand times. Each and every night she tightens the webbing between which this human heart bulges like the dead body of a fly. I attached myself eternally to Ariana when I grasped her throat with her own silk. Now Arachne has bound herself to me eternally with her own thread by strangling my heart.

By way of this mysterious bridge, I am able to visit the Kingdom of the Spiders at midnight, where she is Queen. I am obliged to cross this Hell so that I might, later, find myself beneath the glow of the stars.

There the Spiders of the Woods run with luminous bulbs upon their legs. The Mygalomorphae have eight terrible, sparkling, eyes; bristling with fur, they melt upon me as I make my way along the paths. Around the ponds, where the Water Spiders tremble, rising furious upon their long legs, I am dragged into the whirling rounds that the Tarantulas dance. The Diadem Spiders watch me from the centre of their grey circles, all crisscrossed with rays. The innumerable facets of their eyes fall upon me, like a game of mirrors meant to entrap skylarks, and they fascinate me. Passing beneath the taluses, viscous veils tickle my face. Velvety monsters with quick legs await me, hidden away in the thickets.

But Queen Mab is less powerful than my Queen Arachne. For she has the power to let me ride in her marvellous chariot which runs along a thread. Her cage is made of the hard shell of a gigantic Mygalomorph, bejewelled with sculpted cabochons, hewn in her eyes of black diamond. The axels are the articulated legs of a great Harvest Spider. Transparent wings, with rose windows of veins, raise her, churning the air with rhythmic pulses. We fly for hours; then I collapse suddenly, exhausted by the wound upon my chest where Arachne unceasingly burrows her pointed lips.

In my nightmares, I see chests dotted with eyes bending over me and I flee before coarse legs that bear nets.

Now I feel distinctly the two knees of Arachne sliding upon my ribs; and the gurgling of my blood rising to her mouth. My heart will soon be desiccated; it shall then remain swaddled in her prison of white thread — and I will flee across the Kingdom of the Spiders towards the dazzling trellis of stars. By the silken cord cast down by Arachne, I will flee with her — and I will leave you — poor fools — a pale corpse with a tuft of blond hair to be tousled by the morning wind.

FORMICA SECONDA

TAV: 27

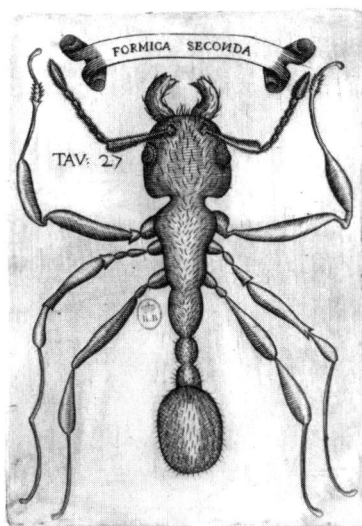

The Dream of Akinosuké

LAFCADIO HEARN

In the district called Toïchi of Yamato Province, there used to live a *gōshi* named Miyata Akinosuké... [Here I must tell you that in Japanese feudal times there was a privileged class of soldier-farmers, — free-holders, — corresponding to the class of yeomen in England; and these were called *gōshi*.]

In Akinosuké's garden there was a great and ancient cedar-tree, under which he was wont to rest on sultry days. One very warm afternoon he was sitting under this tree with two of his friends, fellow-*gōshi*, chatting and drinking wine, when he felt all of a sudden very drowsy, — so drowsy that he begged his friends to excuse him for taking a nap in their presence. Then he lay down at the foot of the tree, and dreamed this dream: —

He thought that as he was lying there in his garden, he saw a procession, like the train of some great daimyō descending a hill near by, and that he got up to look at it. A very grand procession it proved to be, — more imposing than anything of the kind which he had ever seen before; and it was advancing toward his dwelling. He observed in the van of it a number of young men richly apparelled, who were drawing a great lacquered palace-carriage, or *gosho-guruma,* hung with bright blue silk. When the procession arrived within a short distance of the house it halted; and a richly dressed man — evidently a person of rank — advanced from it, approached Akinosuké, bowed to him profoundly, and then said: —

"Honoured Sir, you see before you a *kérai* [vassal] of the *Kokuō* of Tokoyo.[1] My master, the King, commands me to greet you in his august name, and to place myself wholly at your disposal. He also bids me inform you that he augustly desires your presence at the palace. Be therefore pleased immediately to enter this honourable carriage, which he has sent for your conveyance."

Upon hearing these words Akinosuké wanted to make some fitting reply; but he was too much astonished and embarrassed for speech; — and in the same moment his will seemed to melt away from him, so that he could only do as the kérai bade him. He entered the carriage; the kérai took a place beside him, and made a signal; the drawers, seizing the silken ropes, turned the great vehicle southward; — and the journey began.

In a very short time, to Akinosuké's amazement, the carriage stopped in front of a huge two-storied gateway (*rōmon*), of a Chinese style, which he had never before seen. Here the *kérai* dismounted, saying, "I go to announce the honourable arrival," — and he disappeared. After some little waiting, Akinosuké saw two noble-looking men, wearing robes of purple silk and high caps of the form indicating lofty rank, come from the gateway. These, after having respectfully saluted him, helped him to descend from the carriage, and led him through the great gate and across a vast garden, to the entrance of a palace whose front appeared to extend, west and east, to a distance of miles. Akinosuké was then shown into a reception-room of wonderful size and splendour. His guides conducted him to the place of honour, and respectfully seated themselves apart; while serving-maids, in costume of ceremony, brought refreshments. When Akinosuké had partaken of the refreshments, the two purple-robed attendants bowed low before him, and addressed him in the following words, — each speaking alternately, according to the etiquette of courts: —

"It is now our honourable duty to inform you... as to the reason of your having been summoned hither... Our master, the King, augustly desires that you become his son-in-law;... and it is his wish and command that you shall wed this very day... the August Princess, his maiden-daughter... We shall soon conduct you to the presence-chamber... where His Augustness even now is waiting to receive you... But it will be necessary that we first invest you... with the appropriate garments of ceremony."[2]

Having thus spoken, the attendants rose together, and proceeded to an alcove containing a great chest of gold lacquer. They opened the chest, and took from it various robes and girdles of rich material, and a *kamuri*, or regal headdress. With these they attired Akinosuké as befitted a princely bridegroom; and he was then conducted to the presence-room, where he saw the *Kokuō* of Tokoyo seated upon the *daiza*,[3] wearing a high black cap of state, and robed in robes of yellow silk. Before the *daiza*, to left and right, a multitude of dignitaries sat in rank, motionless and splendid as images in a temple; and Akinosuké, advancing into their midst, saluted the king with the triple prostration of usage. The king greeted him with gracious words, and then said: —

"You have already been informed as to the reason of your having been summoned to Our presence. We have decided that you shall become the adopted husband of Our only daughter; — and the wedding ceremony shall now be performed."

As the king finished speaking, a sound of joyful music was heard; and a long train of beautiful court ladies advanced from behind a curtain to conduct Akinosuké to the room in which his bride awaited him.

The room was immense; but it could scarcely contain the multitude of guests assembled to witness the wedding ceremony. All bowed down before Akinosuké as he took his place, facing the King's daughter, on the kneeling-cushion prepared for him. As a maiden of heaven the bride appeared to be; and her robes were beautiful as a summer sky. And the marriage was performed amid great rejoicing.

Afterwards the pair were conducted to a suite of apartments that had been prepared for them in another portion of the palace; and there they received the congratulations of many noble persons, and wedding gifts beyond counting.

🐜 🐜 🐜

Some days later Akinosuké was again summoned to the throne-room. On this occasion he was received even more graciously than before; and the King said to him: —

"In the southwestern part of Our dominion there is an island called Raishū. We have now appointed you Governor of that island. You will find the people loyal and docile; but their laws have not yet been brought into proper accord with the laws of Tokoyo; and their customs have not been properly regulated. We entrust you with the duty of improving their social condition as far as may be possible; and We desire that you shall rule them with kindness and wisdom. All preparations necessary for your journey to Raishū have already been made."

So Akinosuké and his bride departed from the palace of Tokoyo, accompanied to the shore by a great escort of nobles and officials; and they embarked upon a ship of state provided by the king. And with favouring winds they safety sailed to Raishū, and found the good people of that island assembled upon the beach to welcome them.

Akinosuké entered at once upon his new duties; and they did not prove to be hard. During the first three years of his governorship he was occupied chiefly with the framing and the enactment of laws; but he had wise counsellors to help him, and he never found the work unpleasant. When it was all finished, he had no active duties to perform, beyond attending the rites and ceremonies ordained by ancient custom. The country was so healthy and so fertile that sickness and want were unknown; and the people were so good that no laws were ever broken. And Akinosuké dwelt and ruled in Raishū for twenty years more, — making in all twenty-three years of sojourn, during which no shadow of sorrow traversed his life.

But in the twenty-fourth year of his governorship, a great misfortune came upon him; for his wife, who had borne him seven children, — five boys and two girls, — fell sick and died. She was buried, with high pomp, on the summit of a beautiful hill in the district of Hanryōkō; and a monument, exceedingly splendid, was placed upon her grave. But Akinosuké felt such grief at her death that he no longer cared to live.

Now when the legal period of mourning was over, there came to Raishū, from the Tokoyo palace, a *shisha*, or royal messenger. The *shisha* delivered to Akinosuké a message of condolence, and then said to him: —

"These are the words which our august master, the King of Tokoyo, commands that I repeat to you: 'We will now send you back to your own people and country. As for the seven children, they are the grandsons and granddaughters of the King, and shall be fitly cared for. Do not, therefore, allow your mind to be troubled concerning them.'"

On receiving this mandate, Akinosuké submissively prepared for his departure. When all his affairs had been settled, and the ceremony of bidding farewell to his counsellors and trusted officials had been concluded, he was escorted with much honour to the port. There he embarked upon the ship sent for him; and the ship sailed out into the blue sea, under the blue sky; and the shape of the island of Raishū itself turned blue, and then turned grey, and then vanished forever... And Akinosuké suddenly awoke — under the cedar-tree in his own garden!...

For a moment he was stupefied and dazed. But he perceived his two friends still seated near him, — drinking and chatting merrily. He stared at them in a bewildered way, and cried aloud, —

"How strange!"

"Akinosuké must have been dreaming," one of them exclaimed, with a laugh. "What did you see, Akinosuké, that was strange?"

Then Akinosuké told his dream, — that dream of three-and-twenty years' sojourn in the realm of Tokoyo, in the island of Raishū; — and they were astonished, because he had really slept for no more than a few minutes.

One *gōshi* said: —

"Indeed, you saw strange things. We also saw something strange while you were napping. A little yellow butterfly was fluttering over your face for a moment or two; and we watched it. Then it alighted on the ground beside you, close to the tree; and almost as soon as it alighted there, a big, big ant came out of a hole and seized it and pulled it down into the hole. Just before you woke up, we saw that very butterfly come out of the hole again, and flutter over your face as before. And then it suddenly disappeared: we do not know where it went."

"Perhaps it was Akinosuké's soul," the other *gōshi* said; — "certainly I thought I saw it fly into his mouth... But, even if that butterfly was Akinosuké's soul, the fact would not explain his dream."

"The ants might explain it," returned the first speaker. "Ants are queer beings — possibly goblins... Anyhow, there is a big ant's nest under that cedar-tree."

"Let us look!" cried Akinosuké, greatly moved by this suggestion. And he went for a spade.

The ground about and beneath the cedar-tree proved to have been excavated, in a most surprising way, by a prodigious colony of ants. The ants had furthermore built inside their excavations; and their tiny constructions of straw, clay, and stems bore an odd resemblance to miniature towns. In the middle of a structure considerably larger than the rest there was a marvellous swarming of small ants around the body of one very big ant, which had yellowish wings and a long black head.

"Why, there is the King of my dream!" cried Akinosuké; "and there is the palace of Tokoyo!... How extraordinary!... Raishū ought to lie somewhere southwest of it — to the left of that big root... Yes! — here it is!... How very strange! Now I am sure that I can find the mountain of Hanryōkō, and the grave of the princess."

In the wreck of the nest he searched and searched, and at last discovered a tiny mound, on the top of which was fixed a water-worn pebble, in shape resembling a Buddhist monument. Underneath it he found — embedded in clay — the dead body of a female ant.

ENDNOTES

1   This name "Tokoyo" is indefinite. According to circumstances it may signify any unknown country, — or that undiscovered country from whose bourn no traveller returns, — or that Fairyland of far-eastern fable, the Realm of Hōrai. The term "*Kokuō*" means the ruler of a country, — therefore a king. The original phrase, *Tokoyo no Kokuō*, might be rendered here as "the Ruler of Hōrai," or "the King of Fairyland."

2   The last phrase, according to old custom, had to be uttered by both attendants at the same time. All these ceremonial observances can still be studied on the Japanese stage.

3   This was the name given to the estrade, or dais, upon which a feudal prince or ruler sat in state. The term literally signifies "great seat."

EPILOGUE: HUMANS

A Friend to the Animals

LÉON BLOY

To the Friend who will come without being awaited.
Eratque cum bestiis, et angeli ministrabant illi.[1]
Saint Mark, Chapter I.

"**I** do not know," the Consoler said to us, "if the word 'story' quite fits what you are about to hear. It is more the memory of a trip, a dated impression, which remains quite clear and quite deep, that I would like to share with you.

It took place in the mountains near la Salette, where, as the Catholics know, the Virgin appeared before two poor children in 1846.

Naturally, we have done all that we can to dishonour this prodigious event, be it through ridicule or slander. But what does it matter?

And so it was that I found myself in that place of pilgrimage, and, from the very first night, energetically defending a man who was, to me, a stranger. He was seated near me at the table of the inn, where he was mercilessly chided by the unflinching sarcasms of the other patrons.

I had even forced one of these brutes, amongst whom were seated two or three ecclesiastics, to beg his pardon.

You know that it is not in my nature to tolerate the oppression of the weak before my eyes. My current client was a character of sad appearance, dressed like a countryman whose simplicity softened me.

They were making fun of him because he was a vegetarian of sorts, refusing to accept the killing of animals and not allowing himself to eat their flesh, under any pretext whatsoever. He would say it to whomsoever might listen, in such a way that no jeer could ever deter him, and we sensed that he would have given his life for this idea.

The next day, the first person that I saw near the miraculous fountain was the man I had defended. He was praying in profound contemplation, and I was able to observe him.

He was a man of vulgar appearance, dressed in an almost wretched way. He must have been more than fifty years old and already bore the marks of an imminent passing.

One could sense that the myriad blows of misfortune had befallen him. His timid, flinching figure would have been, I believe, insignificant, had it not been for an expression of singular joy which seemed to result from an internal congress. I saw his lips move slightly and, sometimes, smile that soft, pale smile possessed by certain idiots or thoughtful beings whose soul is submerged in a gulf of delectation.

His eyes, especially, surprised me. Fixed upon the bronze image of the Lamenting Virgin, they spoke as one hundred mouths would have, as an entire people with mouths of supplication or praise! I imagined — in that divine register where the vibrations of the heart are to be transposed, one day, in sonorous undulations — a peal of acclamations, of amorous meanderings, of thanks, and of desires.

It seemed to me even — and, for years now, I have held on to this impression — that, from the midst of the surrounding mountains, wreathed at that moment in a blinding fog, a thousand strings of light, of limitless softness and delicateness, had come to rest upon the calamitous face of that worshipper, around whom I thought I could see floating the faintest of effluvia...

When he had finished, he came to me, and, as he removed his garb, spoke:

— 'Sir,' he said, 'I would be glad to speak with you for a moment. Would you do me the honour of walking with me for a brief while?'

We went to sit behind the church, at the edge of the plateau, opposite the Obiou, whose snow-strewn peak was still visible beneath the vapours, and, for that instant, dappled with sunlight.

— 'You hurt me greatly last night,' he began. 'I was unable to stop you, unfortunately, and I am greatly pained by it. You do not know me. I am not an individual to be defended. Before, when I did not yet know myself, I defended myself on my own. I was a hero. I killed a friend in a duel over a joke.

Yes, Sir, I killed a being shaped in God's own image, who had not even offended me. They call that a matter of honour! I struck him square in the chest, and he died as he looked at me, without a word... That look has not left me in twenty-five years, and, even now as I speak to you, he is here, just before me, upon that old firmament column...

When I play back that moment in my mind, I am capable of bearing it all. My only consolation and my only hope is that I might be derided by the people, that they might insult me, drag my face through the mud. Those who do, I love them, I bless them 'with all the blessings of here-below', for that, you see, is justice, *true* Justice.

You became angry and used your force needlessly against a man from whose shoes I, surely, am not worthy of scraping the mud. You forced me to pray for him the whole night long, stretched out over the foot of his door, like a corpse, and, this morning, I implored him, by the Five Wounds of our Saviour, to tread upon my face...

Oh! Sir, I beseech you, do not try to justify me. *Do not address me as a human.* For the Love of God, who walked upon this mountain, I ask it of you. Such things can colour an infamy, do you truly believe that I have not already said it to myself, and that others did not tell me, until that day when I realised I was the lowest of murderers?

That man whom I killed had a wife and two children. The wife died of shame, do you see? Myself, I gave a million crowns for the children. If I did not give everything I had, it is only because family reasons, greater than myself, stood in my way. But I promised to live, to my final hour, the life of a beggar.

In doing so, I hoped that peace would return to me, as if the life of a man could be paid for in crowns. It is the money of the princes of the priests that I gave to those poor children, treated like little Judases by the murderer of their own father. Ah! Indeed! Divine peace was never to return, and every day I live my own crucifixion!...

I tell you this, Sir, because you took pity on me and you might feel some sort of esteem towards me. I am too cowardly still to share my story with the world, as I should, no doubt, and as did the great penitents of the Middle Ages.

I wanted to become a Trappist monk, and then a Chartrain brother. Each and all told me that it was not to be my vocation. And so I married so that I might suffer to my heart's content. I took up with an old wretch from the gutter that not even the sailors would touch. She pummels me mercilessly and gorges me on ridicule and ignominy.

With me she wants for nothing, but I have kept safe the ruins of my fortune — which was rather considerable. It is the fortune of the poor, from which I make tiny withdrawals in order to fund my travels. Last year, I was in the Holy Land, and then in Compostella. Today, I am in Salette for the thirtieth time. They must know me. It is here that I have received the greatest help, and I call upon all those who are unhappy to make this pilgrimage. It is the Sinai of Penitence, the Paradise of Pain, and those who do not understand this are right to complain. Myself, I am just starting to understand, and, sometimes, I am granted absolution for an hour or two...'

He stopped, and I refrained from interrupting the flow of his thoughts. I would have been, moreover, essentially incapable of proffering the slightest word that would not have appeared ridiculous in the presence of this willing convict, of this great Stylite of Expiation.

When, after a moment, he resumed his speech, I had the surprise of an unprecedented transformation. In place of that formidably pathetic man who had pulled upon all of the fibres of my heart, in place of that mound of regrets, of that volcano of lamentations spurting his anguish-laden lava every which way, I heard the humble and mysteriously placid voice that I had heard the night before.

If I implored you, for example, to imagine a dying child that you could hear through a wall, it would be absurd, and yet, I cannot think of anything more fitting. In any case, I had the sense of experiencing something that was infinitely rare...

— 'People often mock me,' that voice said, 'about the animals. You saw it yourself. I believe that I can sense in you a man of imagination. You could, consequently, suspect — imagining me as a sort of timorous zealot — that I derive a sort of pleasure from this ridicule. Nothing of the sort. I am truly made this way. I love animals, whatever sort they might be, almost as much as it is possible or permitted to love man.

I have, I admit, occasionally longed to be entirely dumb, so that I might escape entirely the sophisms of pride; but, because this pleasure has remained thus far unsatisfied, I am incapable of ignoring the sort of disdain there could be in this way of feeling, which extends, in my case, all the way to that passion which even the wisest of people have felt.

But is this not a misunderstanding? Could it be that the majority of men have forgotten that, being creatures themselves, they do not have the right to disdain the other side of creation? Saint Francis of Assisi, whom even the atheists admire, described himself as a doting parent, to not only the animals, but also to the stones and brooks, and the just Job was found blameless when he said to the rotten things: You are my family!

...I know that God gave unto us the beasts of the field: but he did not deliver unto us a commandment to devour them in the material sense, and the experiences of the ascetic life, for several millennia now, have proven that man's strength does not reside in that food source. We do not know Universal Love because we do not see the reality beneath the figures...'

He spoke to me at length in this way with a great faith, a great love, and — I beg you believe it — with a marvellous divination of Christian Symbolism that I was far from expecting from him. I owe much to that simple man, who gifted me, in a few exchanges, with the luminous key to the unknown world.

I assure you that he was prodigious when he spoke of the animals. No more of the great, jarring outbursts from his first confession, no more storms, no more painful meteorites. A divine calm, and what candour!

He came alight peacefully, like a small bedside lamp in a place watched over by angels. As I listened to him, I remembered those Beloved Ones who were the first companions of the Seraphim, whose flower-filled hands spread that sweet perfume throughout the West, and I saw as well all the other Saints of yesteryear, whose pitiful feet left us with several grains of sands from Heaven.

The little that I have told you of his words has surely allowed you to see that it was not one of those imbecilic emotions which are perhaps the most disgusting mode of idolatry. The animals were, for him, the alphabetic signs of Ecstasy. In them he read — like the Chosen of whom I have spoken — the only story of interest to him: the sempiternal of the Trinity, which he asked me to spell out in the symbolic characters of Nature.

My ravishment was inexpressible. In his eyes, the empire of the world, lost by that first Disobedient soul, could only be regained by the integral restitution of the old, pillaged order.

— *The animals, he said to me, are, within our hands, the hostages of vanquished celestial Beauty.*

Strange words, whose depth I have not yet measured. Precisely because the Animals are what man has misunderstood and oppressed the most greatly, he thought that one day, God would use them as his instrument for something unimaginable, when the moment would come for him to manifest his Glory.

That is why his tenderness for these creatures was accompanied by a sort of mystical reverence which was rather difficult to characterize through words. He saw in them the unconscious bearers of a sublime Secret that humanity had no doubt lost beneath the crumbling of Eden and which their sad eyes, covered in shadows, could no longer divulge, since that frightening Breach..."

The Consoler said no more. With his elbows propped upon the table and the tips of his fingers pressed against his temples, he stared vaguely before him, with one of those familiar attitudes, as if he were looking for some great bird of prey in the distance, disillusioned to have returned from the hunt empty-handed, an outward reflection of his own melancholy.

— "What became of that man?" one of us asked him.

— "Ah! yes: my story is not yet finished. I never saw him again, and I learned of his death a year later, through one of my compatriots who lives in the same small town as him in Britany, by the sea.

He died in the most terrible way, and thus the way that he desired most, that is to say in his house, beneath the stern gaze of his abominable wife, Xantippe, whom he had chosen deliberately so that she might torture him.

Stricken with paralysis shortly after our meeting, he did not want to be brought to any sort of clinic where he would have risked dying in peace. Having lived as a penitent, he was happier to moan and to die as a penitent.

It seems that his wife forced him to lie in his own excrement... The details are horrible. For a moment, they thought that she may have poisoned him.

It is certain that she must have been looking forward to him dying, hoping to inherit his wealth. But the precautions had been taken for some time, just as he had told me, and the remainder of his wealth passed into the hands of the poor. Naturally the lease of the architect of his agony ended with him.

Now my story has come to its definite end. You see that it was not too complicated. I wanted simply to have you see him such as I saw him: incompletely, alas! an entirely singular human being, such as I am convinced there is not another on this great earth.

Without that all-too-precise letter from my correspondent in Britany, I would be, sometimes, tempted to wonder if all of that had been real, if that meeting was really anything more than a mirage of my mind, a sort of internal refraction of the Miracle of la Salette, which had undergone a modification as it passed through my soul.

The poor man has stayed there, like a parabolic similitude of the great Christianity of the past that our aborted generations no longer want.

For me, he represents the supernatural combination of childishness in Love and of depth in Sacrifice which made up the integral spirit of the first Christians, around whom whirled the hurricane God's pain.

Flouted by the imbeciles and the hypocrites, a self-appointed pauper and sad unto his death, when he looks at himself, betrothed to the myriad torments and the satisfied companion of all the approbates, this man who burned upon the Cross is, in my eyes, the image and the faithful rendering of those defunct times where the earth was like a great ship in the gulfs of Paradise!"

ENDNOTES

1   "and [He] was with the wild beasts, and the angels ministered
     unto Him."

Bibliographical and
Literary Notes

SAM KUNKEL & JESSICA GOSSLING

CHARLES PIERRE BAUDELAIRE (1821–1867) was a pioneering and masterful French poet, critic, translator, and reluctant grandfather of *fin-de-siècle* decadence. The cat poems by Baudelaire in this bestiary are taken from the first edition of his most famous work, *Les Fleurs du mal* [*Flowers of Evil*], first published by Auguste Poulet-Malassis in 1857. The collection faced legal scrutiny due to its controversial themes and was censored for its explicit content, leading to legal consequences for both Baudelaire and his publisher.

HENRY MAXIMILIAN BEERBOHM (1872–1956) was a British essayist, caricaturist, and parodist known for his wit. Beerbohm's style influenced modern satire and he contributed to many publications, including *The Yellow Book* and *Punch* magazine. "'L'Oiseau Bleu": A Painting on Silk by Charles Conder', was first published in the *Saturday Review*, 6 August 1898, and is based on a real painting by Conder, who was an associate of Beerbohm as well as other decadent writers and artists such as Aubrey Beardsley, Ernest Dowson, and Wilde.

EDWARD FREDERIC BENSON (1867–1940) was an English novelist, biographer, short story writer, and historian. He was the fifth child of the Archbishop of Canterbury, Edward White Benson, and is best known for his humorous and satirical novels, particularly the 'Mapp and Lucia' series, set in small English towns and featuring eccentric characters. Benson's works often examine social dynamics and manners with a comedic touch. 'Caterpillars' is taken from his collection, *The Room in the Tower and Other Stories* (1912).

ALGERNON HENRY BLACKWOOD (1869–1951), an English broadcasting narrator, journalist, and author, is known for his influential contributions to supernatural fiction and horror literature. His works often explore themes of the unknown, nature's mysteries, and the unseen forces of the universe. 'The Golden Fly' is taken from his collection *Pan's Garden: A Volume of Nature Stories* (1912).

LÉON BLOY (1846–1917) is singular, within the context of the decadent literary tradition, for his vehement Catholic faith and his perpetual outrage over the state of the world around him. He is the author of numerous novels and collections of stories, as well as his articles, his short-lived literary revue *Le Pal*, and his conferences. First published as part of his novel, *La Femme pauvre*, Bloy published 'L'Ami des Bêtes' ['A Friend to the Animals'] as a stand-alone story in the first edition of his *Histoires désobligeantes* [*Disagreeable Tales*] in 1894.

HECTOR CHAINAYE (1865–1913) was a minor figure within the Belgian Symbolist movement and is best known for his 1890 collection of prose poems, *L'Âme des choses* [*The Soul of Things*]. He was also a prominent member of the Walloon movement in Belgium. 'The Rat' was published by Chainaye in the revue, *La Jeune Belgique* (January 1889).

ALEISTER CROWLEY (1875–1947) was an influential occultist and ceremonial magician who probably needs no introduction. Through works like *The Book of the Law* (1904), he delved into esoteric and notorious topics, and his writings continue to influence modern occultism and alternative spirituality. 'With Dog and Dame: An October Idyll', is taken from *White Stains: The Literary Remains of George Archibald Bishop, A Neuropath of the Second Empire* (1898), an early collection of his erotic poetry, a form he dabbled in throughout his life but, arguably, without much success.

OLIVE CUSTANCE (1874–1944) was a poet and novelist, celebrated for her romantic and lyrical verse, who moved in aristocratic and literary circles. Influenced by the aesthetic movement, her works explore themes of love, nature, and beauty with a delicate and introspective style. 'Peacocks: A Mood', from her 1905 collection *The Blue Bird*, has been read as a tribute to Oscar Wilde and the mood of wistful homoeroticism at the end of the nineteenth century.

MICHAEL FIELD was the pseudonym used by the aunt and niece Katherine Bradley (1846–1914) and Edith Cooper (1862–1913), two Victorian poets and lovers. Known for their lyrical and dramatic poetry, as well as their taboo romantic relationship, they explored themes of love, nature, and mythology with a unique blend of classical and modern influences. 'χελώνη', usually translated as 'A Tortoise', from *Long Ago* (1889) is unusual for the period due to its explicit depiction of female sexuality alongside a mystical form of erotic desire, a cornerstone of Field's work that reaches its peak in their epic collection of elegies for their beloved dog, *Whym Chow: Flame of Love* (1914).

IWAN GILKIN (1858–1924), although he is far from being the best-known writer of his time, was a prominent member of the Belgian Symbolist movement and helped to found the important literary revue, *La Jeune Belgique* — to which he also contributed regularly. Although he tried his hand at all forms of writing, Gilkin is best known today for his poetry, as well as his numerous plays. 'Le Lévrier' ['The Greyhound'] was published in *La Jeune Belgique* in April 1884, and 'Le Phoque' ['The Seal'] in the January 1889 issue of the same revue, before both were published in Gilkin's collection of poetry, *La Nuit* (1897).

REMY DE GOURMONT (1858–1915) was a leading figure in the Idealist movement in France. He is known for his numerous novels and collections of stories, as well as for his abundant essays, correspondences, and for his role as co-founder and editor of the revue, *Le Mercure de France*. 'Sur le seuil' ['Upon the Threshold'] was published in Gourmont's collection of short stories, *Histoires magiques* [*Magical Stories*] (1894).

STANISLAS DE GUAÏTA (1861–1897), a poet and occultist, founded, along with Joséphin Péladan, the Kabbalistic Order of the Rose+Croix in Paris, before breaking away from him over a dispute concerning the degree to which practical magic should be involved in their worship. In addition to publishing multiple texts on the history and practice of magic, Guaïta also penned a number of collections of poetry, including *La Muse noire* [The Black Muse] (1883) which contained 'La Philosophie des Chats' ['The Philosophy of Cats'].

LAFCADIO HEARN (1850–1904) was a writer, journalist, and educator known for his explorations of Japanese culture. Born in Greece and raised in Ireland, he later moved to the United States and eventually settled in Japan. Hearn's creative works, ghost stories, and essays on Japan introduced Western audiences to Japanese folklore, customs, and spirituality, shaping early perceptions of Japan in the West. 'The Dream of

Akinosuké' was published in *Kwaidan: Stories and Studies of Strange Things* (1904). 'Kwaidan' translates from the Japanese as 'weird tales' or 'ghost stories' and the collection provides an insight into Japanese mythology and gothic horror.

VICTOR HUGO (1802 – 1885) is perhaps best known for his novels and as one of the towering figures the French Romantic movement. However, Hugo was also the author of a number of collections of poetry, including *La Légende des Siècles* [*The Legend of the Centuries*], which was published in three separate instalments before being brought together in 1883. 'Au lion d'Androclès' ['To Androcles' Lion'] was the second poem in the first series, published in 1859 while Hugo was in exile. In this vast poetic cycle, designed to trace the history and evolution of humanity, 'To Androcles' Lion' tells the story of the decadence and fall of Rome.

JORIS-KARL HUYSMANS (1848 – 1907) was a prominent French novelist and art critic, best known for his seminal decadent novel, *À rebours* [*Against Nature*] (1884). 'L'Aquarium de Berlin' ['The Berlin Aquarium'] was first published in Huysmans's collection of essays *De Tout* [*A Bit of Everything*] (1902), a compilation of writings on various subjects of interest to him. In this collection, which shows Huysmans's eclectic and varied interests, 'The Berlin Aquarium' stands out for its keen sense of observation and curiosity, as well for his characteristic cynicism and dark humour. Huysmans was the proud owner of several cats: Bibelot [Trinket], Mouche [Fly], and Barre-de-Rouille [Bar of Rust].

GUSTAVE KAHN (1859 – 1936) is known for his contributions to the development and consolidation of free verse poetry as a legitimate genre, as well as for his novels, art criticism, and significant role as both an editor and a contributor to the Symbolist revues of *fin-de-siècle* Paris. Kahn's 'Poem IX', which is also sometimes called 'Les paons' ['The Peacocks'] was first published in his 1887 collection of poetry, *Les Palais nomads* [*The Nomadic Palaces*].

JULES LAFORGUE (1860–1887) was a Franco-Uruguayan poet and critic whose works were influential in the development of Symbolism and Impressionism, and pioneered free verse poetry. He was also a long-time friend of Gustave Kahn. Laforgue wrote 'L'Aquarium' ['The Aquarium'] sometime in the winter of 1885–1886, before publishing it the May 1886 issue of *La Vogue*. It was later adapted and added to his prose poem 'Salomé' which appears in his collection, *Les Moralités légendaires* [*Moral Tales*].

EUGENE LEE-HAMILTON (1845–1907), the brother of the more famous writer Vernon Lee (Violet Paget), wrote his elegant verse mainly during his twenty-year illness, when he was paralyzed, in severe pain, and barely able to speak. 'To My Tortoise Chronos' is collected in *Sonnets of the Wingless Hours* (1894), a harrowing autobiographical sonnet sequence that describes the monotony of his daily life and his preoccupation with his disabled and dying body.

HOWARD PHILLIPS LOVECRAFT (1890–1937) is the only American writer to feature in this collection. Although proudly attached to his home of New England, many of Lovecraft's stories — especially those from early in his career — speak to the degree to which he was influenced by European decadence. Such is the case for 'The Hound' which not only contains an explicit reference to Huysmans, but mirrors the structure of *À rebours* in many ways. Written sometime around 1922, 'The Hound', was first published in *Weird Tales*, 3.2 (February 1924), 50–52.

MAURICE MAETERLINCK (1862–1949) is known as one of the more prominent voices of the Symbolist movement in Belgium. He wrote novels, essays, and collections of poetry as well as a triptych of scientific essays discussing the lives of bees, termites, and ants. 'Ennui' is from his 1912 collection of poetry *Les Serres chaudes* [*Hothouses*].

STÉPHANE MALLARMÉ (1842–1898) was one of the most revered voices of his generation and a fundamental member of the Symbolist movement in France. Mallarmé published 'Le vierge, le vivace et le bel aujourd'hui' ['The virgin, vivacious, and lovely day at hand'] in his 1887 collection of poetry, *Les Poésies de Stéphane Mallarmé*. It has since become one of his most famous sonnets.

GUY DE MAUPASSANT (1850–1893) is most famous for his novella, *Le Horla* [*The Horla*] (1887), but he is also quite well-known for his short stories, many of which take place in his native Normandy. 'Pierrot' was first published in the revue *Le Gaulois* on 1 October 1882 and was subsequently collected in his anthology *Les Contes de la Bécasse* the following year.

CATULLE MENDÈS (1841–1909) is known for his numerous literary contributions to French decadence and his connections to the Parnassians. 'Le Perroquet, histoire sinistre' ['The Parrot, a Dark Tale'] is a story that Mendès revisited at several points throughout his career, and it was first published in the newspaper *Beaumarchais* on 5 December 1880. Subsequently, it was printed in the *Gil Blas* on 12 August 1882 where it appeared simply as 'Le Perroquet'. In 1883, it was included in Mendès's anthology *L'Amour qui rit et l'amour qui pleure* [*The Love that Cries and the Love that Laughs*].

EMILY PFEIFFER (1827–1890) was a Welsh poet, essayist, and philanthropist known for her poetry that often addressed social issues such as women's rights, labour conditions, and humanitarian causes. Pfeiffer's works were notable for their lyrical style and their engagement with contemporary issues, reflecting the social consciousness of her time. 'To a Moth That Drinketh of the Ripe October' was published in her collection *Sonnets and Songs* (1880).

RACHILDE (1860–1953), the pseudonym and preferred identity of Marguerite Vallette-Eymery, was one of the most important female voices of *fin-de-siècle* France. She is known for her prose writings, which often expose the crueller side of human nature, and for her controversial politics and lifestyle — such as her pet sewer rats, Kyrie and Eleison, which she carried on her shoulders when she went out in public. 'Le Tueur de grenouilles' ['The Frog Killer'] was first published in the July–September 1900 issue of the *Mercure de France*, before being collected in *Contes et Nouvelles* [*Tales and Stories*], later that year.

JULES RENARD (1864–1910) is perhaps best remembered for his semi-autobiographical novel, *Poil de carotte* [*Carrot Top*] (1894). Renard (whose surname, it is worth noting in a collection such as this, means 'fox' in French) published both 'Chauves-souris' ['Bats'] and 'La chenille' ['The Caterpillar'] in his 1894 collection *Histoires naturelles* [*Natural Stories*]. Since its first publication, *Histoires naturelles* has been reprinted numerous times, and has been illustrated by several famous artists, including Henri de Toulouse-Lautrec in 1899.

DANTE GABRIEL ROSSETTI (1828–1882) was a multi-talented artist, renowned for his paintings and poetry, and a founding member of the Pre-Raphaelite Brotherhood. His works often depicted themes of love, beauty, and medievalism, embodying the Romantic spirit of the Victorian era, but were also infused with veiled references to a darker, more decadent and sensual sensibility. Rossetti's 'Sunset Wings', which was inspired by a flock of starlings that Rossetti noticed while at Kelmscott with Jane Morris in 1871, was first published in the *Athenaeum* (24 May 1873), before being collected in *Ballads and Sonnets* (1881).

SAKI (1870–1916), the penname of Hector Hugh Munro, was a British writer renowned for his satirical and humorous short stories. His works often featured witty dialogues and ironic twists, satirizing the absurdities of upper-class society. In most of his short story collections, such as *The Chronicles of Clovis* (1912) in which 'Sredni Vashtar' appears, animals are featured extensively.

OLIVE SCHREINER (1855–1920) was a South African writer and feminist known for her novels, essays, and social commentary. Born in Wittebergen, she advocated for women's rights, pacifism, and social justice. Her engagement with decadent ideas, such as intersensoriality and the cultivation of new ways of perceiving reality, can be seen in 'A Dream of Wild Bees (written as a letter to a friend)', in *Dreams*, a collection of personal correspondence and allegories published in 1915.

MARCEL SCHWOB (1867–1905), one of the more singular writers of the 1890s, first published 'Arachne' in the 20 July 1889 issue of *L'Écho de Paris* in *Le Phare de la Loire*. It was later collected in his 1891 collection *Cœur double* [*Double Heart*] and is one of his earliest stories. Schwob kept a number of pets in his Paris apartment, including a dormouse, a squirrel, a snake, and two dogs — a Brussels Griffon and a Shiba Inu, the latter being a gift from the legendary dandy Robert de Montesquiou.

WILLIAM SHARP (1855 – 1905) was a Scottish writer, poet, and mystic, who also wrote under the pseudonym Fiona Macleod, which added an air of mystery to his literary persona. Known for his lyrical and spiritual prose and poetry, Sharp's works explore Celtic folklore, nature, and spirituality. 'The White Peacock' was published in Sharp's self-published book of free-verse poetry, *Sospiri di Roma* (1891).

COUNT ERIC STANISLAUS STENBOCK (1860 – 1895), born in Southwest England and of a Baltic Swedish aristocratic lineage, was described by W. B. Yeats as a 'scholar, connoisseur, drunkard, poet, pervert, most charming of men'. His only short story collection, *Studies of Death* (1894), in which 'The Egg of the Albatross' appears, explores themes of mortality and the afterlife, showcasing his fascination with the macabre and with the symbiotic relationship between humans and animals. He was the owner of numerous pets, including a serpent, a toad, and a dachshund called Trixie.

ARTHUR SYMONS (1865 – 1945) was a British poet, critic, and editor associated with symbolism and decadence. Symons's translations, of Charles Baudelaire and Villiers de l'Isle-Adam to name but two, as well as his own poetry and essays on decadence, contributed significantly to the development of English decadence. In February 1906, following his mental breakdown, Symons and his wife Rhoda adopted a puppy called Api, who died ten months later on Christmas day. Symons's grief is collected in a limited-edition pamphlet entitled *For Api*, published seven years later, which contains memorial verses and a sequence of prose poems.

JOHN TODHUNTER (1839 – 1916) was an Irish poet, playwright, and scholar. He contributed significantly to Irish literary and cultural revival movements, writing poetry that often explored themes of nature, mythology, and spirituality. 'Snake-charm' appears in *Forest Songs and Other Poems* (1881), his fourth collection of poetry.

COUNT VILLIERS DE L'ISLE-ADAM (1838 – 1889) is undeniably one of the most seminal and enigmatic figures of the Symbolist movement. He was revered as much for his prose works as for his pioneering plays. 'Le Tueur des cygnes' ['The Swan Killer'] marks the second appearance of Villiers' character, Tribulat Bonhomet, who first emerged in the short story 'Claire Lenoir' and would also feature in a number of other stories before lending his name to a collection which appeared in 1887. 'Le Tueur des cygnes' was first published in the 26 June 1886 issue of *Le Chat Noir*.

RENÉE VIVIEN (1877 – 1909) was equally skilled in both poetry and prose, and capable of writing in both French and English. She is notorious for her titillating and mysterious lifestyle, such as her stifling decadent apartment that housed her collection of pet frogs, and is the author of a vast catalogue which is significant for its dexterous language, as well as its fiercely independent point of view. 'La Dame a la louve' ['The Lady with the Wolf'] was first published in a collection of the same name in 1904.

JOHN BYRNE LEICESTER WARREN (1835 – 1895) was an English diplomat, scholar, art collector, and poet. He is best known for his archaeological excavations in Greece, particularly at the site of Sparta, where he unearthed significant artifacts. Warren's contributions to classical studies and his efforts in preserving ancient Greek heritage earned him recognition in the academic and archaeological communities. He is less well-known as a poet, and his romantic and lyrical verse often reflected his deep appreciation for nature, history, and classical themes, showcasing his diverse interests beyond his scholarly pursuits. 'The Study of a Spider', appears in *Poems, Dramatic and Lyrical* (1893).

ROSAMUND MARRIOTT WATSON (1860 – 1911), a luminary of late nineteenth-century poetry, wrote under the pseudonyms Graham R. Tomson and Rushworth (or R.) Armytage early in her career. Her poetry is suffused with sensuality and natural beauty alongside a sense of decay and fascination with organic transformation. 'Ballad of the Bird-Bride' was published in her first collection, *A Summer Night and Other Poems* (1889).

OSCAR WILDE (1854–1900) was a leading figure of the Aesthetic Movement in Victorian literature, known for his wit, flamboyant style, and sharp social commentary. Wilde's celebrity status as a playwright and poet was marred by scandal and imprisonment due to his homosexuality, highlighting Victorian society's intolerance. His fairy tales, such as 'The Nightingale and the Rose', published in *The Happy Prince and Other Tales*, illustrated by Walter Crane and Jacomb Hood (David Nutt, 1888), remain timeless classics, blending whimsy with profound themes and moral lessons, showcasing Wilde's versatility as a storyteller.

WILLIAM BUTLER YEATS (1865–1939) was an Irish poet, playwright, and received the Nobel prize for literature in 1923. Known for his mystical and symbolic poetry, he explored themes of mythology, politics, and the human condition, leaving a profound impact on modern poetry and Irish cultural identity. Yeats was one of Crowley's rivals within the London Golden Dawn group, no doubt instigated by Yeats's superior poetic talent, as exemplified in the magisterial poem 'The Wild Swans at Coole', first published in the June 1917 issue of the *Little Review* before becoming the title poem in Yeats's 1917 collection *The Wild Swans at Coole*.

List of Images

The page facing the title page: August Leroux's illustration from J. K. Huysmans, *À rebours* (A. Ferroud, 1920), p. 47. © University of Ottawa, Public Domain.

2.8 Gustave Doré's illustration for Hippolyte Adolphe Taine's *Voyage aux Pyrénées: Troisième édition illustrée par Gustave Doré* (1860) © British Library Digital Store 12271.c.20, Public Domain

2.9 Illustration from Jacques de Sève, *Chat monstrueux à deux têtes*, for *Histoire naturelle générale et particulière* by Buffon (1756) © Bibliothèque nationale de France, Public Domain

2.10 Illustration from Zadock Thompson's *History of Vermont: Natural, Civil, and Statistical* (1853) © British Library Digital Store 010410.ee.14, Public Domain

2.11 Illustration from Zadock Thompson's *History of Vermont: Natural, Civil, and Statistical* (1853) © British Library Digital Store 10410.d.34, Public Domain

2.12 Illustration from Léon Curmer, *Ordre des cheiroptères* (1845–1855) © Bibliothèque nationale de France, Public Domain

3.   BIRDS

3.1 Illustration from Raoul Duffy, *Le Paon*, from *Le Bestiaire ou Cortège d'Apollon* (1919) © Bibliothèque nationale de France, Public Domain

3.2 Illustration from Clara L. Matéaux's *Woodland Romances; or, Fables and Fancies* (1877) © British Library Digital Store 11651.f.1, Public Domain

3.3 Illustration from Anton Seder, 'Illustration no. 27', in *Das Thier in der decorativen Kunst* (Gerlach & Schenk, 1896)

3.4 Illustration from L. P. Vieillot's *Galerie des oiseaux du Cabinet d'histoire naturelle du Jardin du roi* (1834) © Biodiversity Heritage Library Collections QL674.V68, Public Domain

3.5 Illustration from Jemima Blackburn's *Birds from Moidart and elsewhere* (1895) © Biodiversity Heritage Library Collections OCLC: 6347330, Public Domain

3.6 Pierre Roche, *Le Perroquet*, from *Recueil. Œuvre de Pierre Roche* (1897) © Bibliothèque nationale de France, Public Domain

3.7 J. J. Grandville, *Second rêve : une promenade dans le ciel*, from *Le Magasin pittoresque* (1847) © Bibliothèque nationale de France, Public Domain

3.8 Illustration from Bertrand et Barthère's *Comédie de la mort* (1854) © Bibliothèque nationale de France, Public Domain

3.9 Illustration from Carl Harald Eugène Lewenhaupt's *Från Upländsk bygd* (1899) © British Library Digital Store 10281.l.13, Public Domain

3.10 Illustration from Samuel Page Widnall's *A Mystery of Sixty Centuries; or, a Modern St. George and the Dragon* (1889) © British Library Digital Store 012603.cc.24, Public Domain

3.11 Philippe Rousseau, *Le Renard et la Cigogne*, from *Recueil. Œuvre de Philippe Rousseau* (1859) © Bibliothèque nationale de France, Public Domain

3.12 Illustration from Prideaux John Selby's *Illustrations of British Ornithology* (1819) © Biodiversity Heritage Library Collections QL674.S46 1819, Public Domain

3.13 Maurice Pillard Verneuil, *Perroquet. Aigle. Cygnes et iris.*, from *L'Animal dans la decoration* (1897) © Bibliothèque nationale de France, Public Domain

3.14 Illustration from Robert Brown's *The Countries of the World: being a popular description of the various continents, islands, rivers, seas, and peoples of the globe* (1876) © British Library Digital Store 10006.ff.1, Public Domain

3.15 Illustration from Francis C. Woodworth's *Stories about Birds, with Pictures to Match* (1851) © Biodiversity Heritage Library Collections QL676.W88Z, Public Domain

4. FISH & HERPTILES

4.1 Illustration from Jean le Rond d'Alembert and Denis Diderot's *Encyclopédie, ou Dictionnaire raisonné des sciences, des arts et des métiers Henry Martyn* (1768) © Bibliothèque nationale de France, Public Domain

4.2 Illustration from Robert Brown's *The Countries of the World: being a popular description of the various continents, islands, rivers, seas, and peoples of the globe* (1894) © British Library Digital Store 10025.ee.15, Public Domain

4.3 Illustration from Emmanuel Ratoin's *Nos nouvelles colonies: Le Congo* (1890) © British Library Digital Store 010096. ee.14, Public Domain

4.4 Illustration from 'Proceedings of the general meetings for scientific business of the Zoological Society of London', *London Academic Press* 6 vols (1846-60) © Biodiversity Heritage Library Collections QL1.J88, Public Domain

4.5 'La tortue-bijou', from *L'Illustration*, 2864 (15 January 1898), p. 53 © Samuel Kunkel Collection

STRANGE ATTRACTOR PRESS
2025